HAUNTED LOVE

HAUNTED LOVE

Tales of Ghostly Soulmates,
Spooky Suitors, and Eternal Love

Chris Gonsalves

Guilford, Connecticut

To buy books in quantity for corporate use
or incentives, call **(800) 962-0973**
or e-mail **premiums@GlobePequot.com.**

Text design: Sheryl P. Kober

Library of Congress Cataloging-in-Publication Data is available on file.

ISBN 978-0-7627-5276-8

Printed in the United States of America

10 9 8 7 6 5 4 3 2 1

To Hal Peterson, whose own ghost makes an appearance at the end of this work. It's the most we've talked in a long time, old friend, and I'm sorry. And to Carrie L. Stephens, a young woman I never met, whose tragic death sparked my love affair with writing.

CONTENTS

ACKNOWLEDGMENTS

Special thanks go to Ken and Heidi Montigny, Mike and Christine Goulart, Mickey and Andree Goulart, Myles Goulart, Paul Berberian, Blanche Pepin, Monique Bradley, all the folks at the Kinsale Inn, Dennis Fisher, David and Ann Humphrey, Mike Zimmerman, Rob O'Regan, the Pasta House, David Sendler, Donna Scaglione, Max and Sam Burt, Scot Petersen, Eric Schmidt and Sergey Brin, Mattapoisett Congregational Church, Lawrence Walsh, Chris Ruddy, Cable Neuhaus, Ken Williams and the whole gang at Newsmax, Carmen Nobel, Ian Anderson, Martin Guitars, the City of Palm Beach Gardens, Sebastian's, Greg Brown, Pa Raffa, Lexington Green, Richie and everyone at Turk's Seafood, North Lake Presbyterian Church, Christ Fellowship Gardens Campus, Penn State, the Gators, the Thirsty Turtle and the Brass Ring, the 2004 Boston Red Sox, and, of course, Bootsy and Muffin.

AUTHOR'S NOTE

The name of some individuals in this book have been changed either at their request or to protect their privacy. Some of the events have been dramatized or modified for the sake of clarity or continuity.

Many of these stories are based on legend, rumor, hearsay, gossip, and the occasional distant or foggy memory. The author makes no claim as to the authenticity of any story contained here, except that, in every case, the best available sources believe them to be true.

The majority of the locations mentioned here are private properties, and some may have changed ownership since the publication of this book. Please remember to be respectful of personal privacy should you decide to explore these ghost stories on your own.

INTRODUCTION

The Heart of a Ghost

Love is a scary thing.

We expose our hearts and bare our souls all on the outside chance that our affections may be returned in kind. When they are not, it can be crushing. But when they are, that's when romance can turn downright otherworldly. Hearts race, breath quickens, senses are set ablaze; it's all part of what makes love so frighteningly grand. As the French philosopher François de La Rochefoucauld, author of the famed *Maximes*, said four centuries ago: "It is with true love as it is with ghosts; everyone talks about it, but few have seen it."

Small wonder, then, that love has often been linked with spirits that transcend mortality. Popular fiction is filled with references to love's power to leave its mark on our mortal plane long after the lovers are gone. Millions wept in the summer of 1990 when Patrick Swayze played Sam Wheat, a murdered man so deeply in love with his girlfriend, portrayed by Demi Moore, that he refused to be carted off to heaven until he could both protect her and finally express his undying love for her. The movie, *Ghost*, went on to great critical acclaim and much financial success. The film's iconic potter's wheel encounter between Moore and Swayze is rated the No. 1 movie love scene of all time by *Premier Magazine*.

Moore's character, Molly, owes a great deal to perhaps the most famous haunted lover in the history of modern fiction—Edgar Allan Poe's unnamed narrator in his poem "The

Raven." In both, we see earthbound mourners torn between a desire to forget and an obsession to remember their dead lovers. They at once crave any sign at all from their beloved in the Afterlife, even as they remain convinced that their ghostly encounters are sure indication of a descent into madness. In complicated meter and rhyme scheme, Poe's "The Raven" tells the tale of a young scholar mourning the loss of "the rare and radiant maiden whom the angels named Lenore." Through a spooky encounter with a supernatural talking bird, the young man discovers the depth of both his sadness and his love, and is left with the discovery that he will always suffer because of his loss. Or as Poe put it so poetically, "and my soul from out that shadow that lies floating on the floor shall be lifted—Nevermore."

The poem, Poe's most famous work by far, was a sensation in its day. It was even committed to memory by none other than President Abraham Lincoln. Nobody is really sure why. Lincoln was a fan of great writing, and he also believed memorizing brilliant passages of prose and poetry helped him with his substantial oratory skills. But it's equally possible that Lincoln was a bit of a romantic. He certainly believed in the power of love to transcend life. He recited William Knox's poem "Mortality: Oh, Why Should the Spirit Be Proud?" so often that many people mistakenly thought Lincoln had written the piece.

Both Shakespeare's shortest play (*Macbeth*) and his longest (*Hamlet*) have as their central feature disastrous love stories and interceding spirits. Even the Bard himself knew that love was force enough to power tyranny, treason, murder, suicide, and insanity.

For a more lowbrow look at the mysteries—and dark comedy—of love across the boundaries of the living, there's always *The Ghost and Mrs. Muir*. Both the successful 1947 feature film and subsequent 1960s television series tell the story of a vivacious young widow who moves into a centuries-old oceanfront home and begins a spirited affair with the ghost of a long-dead sea captain. The campy story is more funny than spooky, but its premise makes great use of the concept that love, understanding, forgiveness, and yes, even passion, cannot be contained by the grave.

Maybe the most clever treatment of the subject comes from author Jonathan Carroll, whose 2008 novel *The Ghost in Love* paints a modern and darkly humorous picture of a ghost sent from heaven to retrieve the soul of a dead man, who instead falls in love with the man's wife. Though he's a gourmet chef and can communicate fluently with the family dog, the ghost finds it very difficult to get his passions across to a living woman. In the end, as one would imagine, love prevails, though not as it was intended.

By now you recognize the thread. Whether it's Carroll, Poe, or Patrick Swayze, the message is the same: You just can't kill love.

All of these bits of popular culture draw their breath from countless tales of haunted romance that are as old as storytelling itself. That's because the conceit of undying love has a basis in real life. It's not just in fiction that dead lovers get to rejoin the mortal world to finish what death rent asunder. When it comes to this deepest of all human bonds, true stories abound of mysterious encounters—spirited sounds and ghostly visions—in the places where true romance burned brightest. In our world, the briefer and hotter the affair, it seems, the more likely some specter will continue to search for a lost romance. They are stories of the tenderness, heartbreak, and raw emotion that accompany most passionate love affairs, as well as the chilling encounters with the ghosts these often ill-fated romances leave behind.

Haunted Love is a collection of such tales. In settings ranging from tropical South Florida to exotic South Korea and a dozen places in between, there are true, ongoing stories that can both touch the heart and tingle the spine. There's the story of the high-born, widowed innkeeper who fell into league with bootleggers and continues to keep watch for the man she loved, long after he drowned in the stormy Atlantic. A world away, in a sleepy New England town, a jilted teenage lover continues to torment anyone who ventures near the bridge where she took her own life.

You'll read of an English train haunted by the ghost of a jealous husband, and a spooky rooming house in Virginia that was once the scene of forbidden love between a Confederate nurse and a Union soldier. In nearly every case, the spirits return to seek closure to a romance that was ended unfairly or too soon. Much is made in the world of ghost hunting about the spirits of the undead who are restless because of some perceived injustice; a wrongful conviction or unsolved murder, perhaps. However, it would seem there are no greater injustices—and no better reasons for ghosts to keep their horrific earthy vigils—than unrequited romance and unfinished love.

And so, where the heart has been, there too are spirits.

Again, in the words of La Rochefoucauld: "Love, like fire, cannot continue to exist without continual motion; both cease to live so soon as they cease to hope . . . or to fear." Hope or fear. When it comes to *Haunted Love*, our ghosts deliver plenty of both.

HAUNTED LOVE

Chapter 1
The Lady with
the Lantern

In historic St. Augustine, Florida, a place known as America's oldest city, mysterious lights frequently shine from the widow's walk of a weathered old inn. It's just the old widow herself, still watching out for the outlaw-lover she lost to the sea.

They were from two entirely different worlds.

Anna was a high-born member of St. Augustine's elite. A raven-haired beauty, well-mannered and gracefully aged, she was known all around the historic port city as a demure widow who busied herself with running the quaint waterfront inn she'd taken over after her husband died. Then, as now, Anna's family ran St. Augustine. The men were financiers and captains of industry. The women held sway over the social order in America's oldest city. Charming Anna fit right in among them.

George was a hustler. A petty thief and con man, he'd graduated to rumrunner when Prohibition presented America's crooks with a robust new revenue stream in 1920. George landed in St. Augustine in early 1923 mostly by chance. He found this stretch of northern Florida's convoluted Atlantic coastline, from Rattlesnake Island to Ponte Vedra, the perfect setting for his budding career. The overgrown coves along Mantanzas Bay and the treacherous waters of the Conch Island inlet gave George and his cohorts ample cover from federal agents as they ferried illegal Cuban booze from

the Bahamas into the United States. It was a lucrative enter-
prise, as long as you kept from being pinched by the cops.
And as long as you had a place to fence the illegal hooch.
Those two things were rarely a problem for George any lon-
ger. It was here that the two entirely different worlds of
George and Anna intersected.

Their pairing was so unlikely that few would have imagined it or believed it possible. Anna was thinking exactly
that as she fell into George's arms on a humid June night
in 1926. There, in the inky blackness of Vilano Beach, she
kissed him for the first time. The night breeze riffled through
the sabal palms overhead. She'd fallen for him. She loved
him. She told him so.

"When will you go again?" she asked.

"We leave in the morning," he said. "We'll be back just
after midnight a week from tomorrow. You'll be ready?"

He couldn't see her smile in the darkness. She pulled
him closer.

"Always," she said. "You know I'll always be ready."

Anna kissed her young bandit-lover goodnight. This
was a dark, forbidden thing, like nothing she'd ever known
before. The very thought of it thrilled her. She started away,
then turned back to him quickly and brought her lips close
to his ear to whisper over the roaring Atlantic.

"Watch for the light, my love. Follow the light."

Back in her room at the Bayfront Boarding House, Anna's
head spun with this latest twist in what was already a surreal
experience for her. The rich and powerful of St. Augustine
would be beside themselves if they ever discovered that this
respected and cultured elderly woman had fallen into league
with bootleggers. What would they say if they learned she'd
turned her own hotel into a sort of speakeasy and a waypoint

for the transport of illegal booze? The truth was, the ruse had been going on for several months now, ever since George and his gang approached her with the prospect of sharing their valuable stash of liquor with her in exchange for shelter and information. It had been going quite nicely.

She told herself at the time it was just a business arrangement. Sure, the inn did a fair business, but the extra money she could earn selling alcohol to wealthy tourists wouldn't hurt. And Anna had something much more valuable to offer George's gang than merely a place to hide out and a way to fence their booty. The Bayfront Boarding House had become a favorite haunt of the federal agents who patrolled the Florida coast looking for bootleggers. Like good, organized bureaucrats, they always made arrangements days in advance. Anna was the one person in all of St. Augustine who knew when it was safe to come ashore with a boatload of Cuban rum.

"It's just for the money. Just for a little while," Anna had told herself over and over.

But lately every time she looked at George, really looked at him—a scruffy, wiry, tough guy who spent every waking minute staying a step ahead of those who hunted him— her Southern heart skipped a beat. Now she'd told him she loved him. It wasn't about the money anymore. She wasn't a business partner or a conspirator. For the first time since her husband had passed away, she was a woman looking out for her man.

A spring in her step, Anna skipped along the brick walkway toward the Bayfront's coach house. She plucked a fresh hibiscus bloom and tucked it in her graying hair. Everything in the ancient city seemed newer, brighter. Anna beamed as she surveyed her property, a marvel of Mediterranean revival architecture designed by Gould T. Butler and built in 1914 on prime real estate in the heart of St. Augustine. The twenty-three-room inn, originally named the Mantanzas Hotel, was adorned with wraparound porches that offered sweeping views of the bay and the nearby seventeenth-century Spanish fort of Castillo de San Marcos. It was as beautiful as it was strategic, she knew. Anna spent her days after that windswept kiss with George giddily greeting guests and impatiently fussing over details around the inn. As she passed by the reception area, her desk clerk called out.

"Miss Anna. A moment please."

Anna skipped over to the front desk, still buzzing with nervous energy.

"Miss Anna, we just received a wire from up north. From the Treasury Department. The lawmen from Washington would like two rooms day after next. They'll be here three nights. You asked me to tell you if . . ."

The clerk stopped as Anna's face went slack and white.

"Are you all right, ma'am?"

"Of course. Of course, I'm fine."

She composed herself.

"Tell the agents they're welcome, as always," Anna said. "Give them the rooms on the first floor rear, and be sure to let me know as soon as they arrive."

She hurried away from the desk before her fear betrayed her. She struggled to keep her thoughts together. She could not let her emotions scuttle their plans.

It's not as though Anna hadn't been through this drill dozens of times. In fact, she and George had a nearly foolproof system for avoiding the G-men. Whenever George and his crew were due back in St. Augustine, Anna would stand on the Bayfront Boarding House's rooftop deck, up against the pillastered railing, with a lantern in hand. If the coast was clear, she would hold the lantern steady. If the revenuers were afoot, Anna would wave her lantern from side to side. George and his fellow bootleggers would sail past the harbor entrance and hole up on one of the barrier islands until the heat was off. They'd worked the scheme successfully on many nights. Still, this time was different. Her newfound love for George had amplified everything. She'd been nervous before, but now she was truly afraid. Afraid her lover would get caught, afraid he'd get hurt, afraid she'd slip up and let him down. She had to focus.

Anna spent the next few days sequestered in her room at the Bayfront. When the federal agents arrived, she greeted them curtly and showed them to their room. She asked if they would like seats reserved for dinner during their stay. They politely declined. Anna knew exactly what that meant. It was a clear sign they'd be on the prowl along the St. Augustine waterfront in the evenings. That bit of knowledge set Anna's plans into motion. She stepped out onto the porch to get some air and watched small boats criss-cross the bay in the twilight. A cool, moist wind was picking up from the southwest; she could hear it in the rustling palms. It was a sure sign that foul weather was on the way. *That storm is probably already chasing George home,* she thought.

"Be safe, my love," Anna whispered into the sea breeze. "Watch for the light."

Just before midnight on the night George was to return, Anna strolled casually around the back porch by the windows of the rooms where the federal agents were lodged. Her heart sank. The quarters were dark, empty. The lawmen were clearly on patrol, lying in wait for men like George. The wind that foretold bad weather days ago was now a full-on gale. She climbed the stairs to her rooftop perch, lantern in hand, and braced herself against the howling wind. The rain stung her eyes as she tried to scan the harbor. She could only imagine what it was like for George, in his small boat laden with cases of illegal booze, trying to navigate the treacherous inlet in a gathering storm. As she began to uncover her lantern, she was torn. If she warned George off by waving the lamp, he'd be forced to stay at sea in the gale. If she held her light steady, he'd be safe, but caught.

She held her breath and raised the lantern above her head. She held it steady against the wind and driving rain. She thought of George, her man, her wild, untamed lover, captured and caged. It would break him. It would break her. She began to swing the lantern, in slow arcs at first. Then, more urgently, she waved the lamp back and forth. Her tears mixed with the rain. After thirty minutes she quit, knowing George had seen the warning and stayed in the roiling sea, but still hoping that, perhaps, he hadn't.

The next day there was no sign of George or the federal agents. Anna paced the halls of the Bayfront Boarding House, snapping impatiently at her staff and feeling as though she'd go mad if she didn't see her lover come running across the St. Augustine pier and up the front steps soon. Early in the afternoon, the G-men, bleary-eyed, wet, and haggard from a full night of surveillance in the tropical storm, returned to the hotel.

"Any luck, gentlemen?" Anna asked as nonchalantly as possible. She fiddled with papers at the front desk, trying to look busy, occupied. Most of all trying to appear calm.

"No, ma'am. We didn't catch any fish," one of the agents said. "But you should have seen the one that got away."

The agents exchanged wry smiles and headed back to their rooms. Anna managed to stay collected until she got to her own chamber, where she sank into a chair and sobbed deeply. She stayed in her room the entire night and into the next day. From her balcony she saw the agents trudge from the hotel, bags in hand, making their way back to Washington. Anna cursed them under her breath.

Weeks went by with no word about George. Finally, after an exceptionally high tide that September, beachcombers found the splintered remains of his boat on one of St. Augustine's barrier islands. No trace of George or his crew was ever found, but folks across the city assumed the ruffian they'd seen hanging around the Bayfront Boarding House had drowned in the storm. When they saw how inconsolable Anna had become around the same time, tongues began to wag. Perhaps George was more than just a questionable regular guest in an otherwise respectable hotel run by one of St. Augustine's most upstanding women.

Anna spent much of the rest of her days in morose solitude in and around the Bayfront Boarding House. She may have been sad, but she'd amassed a small fortune through her joint venture with George and his bootlegging buddies. She was a millionaire, in fact, but it wasn't enough to buy the old woman's happiness. She never mentioned George to anyone. When she passed away peacefully a decade later, she took her lover's memory quietly to her grave in the nearby Huguenot Cemetery. And there she stayed, at least for a while.

On an April evening in 2001, Luis Gomes-Real was steering his shrimp boat through a thickening fog back into Mantanzas Bay. After a lifetime of fishing the waters off St. Augustine, he knew the landmarks and the features of the local coast the way most folks know the layout of their own living rooms. So he was startled by a flashing light coming from off his starboard bow in an area he was certain was the row of simple, wood-front shops and inns of the city's historic Avenida Martinez. So, what was it? Had the fog confused him? Was he turned around? If that light was really the Anastasia Island Lighthouse, he was headed in the wrong direction and in imminent danger of running aground. He cut his engines and let the trawler drift until the source of the light became clearer. Sure enough, the steady flashing beams were coming from atop the old Bayfront Boarding House, a place that had recently been fixed up and turned into the Casablanca Inn. Luis took out his binoculars to get a better look.

It was a woman. Or more the shape of a woman, as gray and translucent as the fog that was swirling around her. The specter was waving a lantern above her head, side to side, back and forth, as if warning someone to stay away. The fisherman got a chill up his spine. He checked his navigation equipment one more time to make sure he was where he thought he was. When he looked back toward the Casablanca, the light, and the ghostly figure wielding it, were gone.

Luis docked his boat and unloaded his catch, forgetting about the experience. A few weeks later, he and a few waterfront regulars were tipping a few in the Mill Top Tavern when someone at the bar said they'd nearly gone aground in the bay after being distracted by a weird flashing light coming from an area just north of the Bridge of Lions.

"That's the Lady with the Lantern, son," one of the shrimpers chimed in. "Best not to be looking toward the Casablanca at night. You'll end up on a sandbar right quick."

Everyone laughed. Luis was dumbfounded.

"You've seen this?" he asked.

"Of course," one of the grizzled fishermen told him. "The old widow is signaling her boyfriend. Trouble is, they're both dead. You will be too if you get fooled by that crazy light."

"Ain't love grand?" another man said to Luis, raising his glass. Luis returned the toast. He was a new member of a different sort of fraternity now: a group of seamen who share the secret of the Lady of the Lantern.

Not long after Luis's spooky experience, an elderly couple, Bob and Irene McMartin, traveled from Ocala, Florida, to stay at the Casa de la Paz, a bed-and-breakfast next to the Casablanca. Their trip was uneventful until the pair retired for the second night of their three-night stay.

After a full day of touring America's oldest European-style city, walking in the footsteps of Spanish explorers Juan Ponce de Leon and Pedro Menendez de Aviles, who built a colony in St. Augustine more than a half century before the Pilgrims arrived at Plymouth Rock, the McMartins were ready for a peaceful night in their cozy room.

"I doubt there's anything in this old city we haven't seen," Bob told Irene as he stretched out on the Casa de la Paz's plush four-poster bed.

He was wrong.

The pair had been asleep for only an hour or so when something woke Bob up. He struggled first to figure out where he was, then, when he got his bearings in the strange hotel room, he focused on what had roused him. There was a strangely bright, flashing light filling the room. He squinted, trying to find its source. Bob quickly realized the light wasn't coming from inside the room, but rather was shining in through the window that faced the inn next door. He assumed some hooligan was playing with a flashlight. Bob, a strapping, no-nonsense former police detective from New Hampshire, strode over to the window ready to throw it open and give some joker a piece of his mind.

What he saw when he got to the window, however, made his blood run cold. Through the balusters of the widow's walk on the adjacent inn, Bob saw a ghostly woman in a flowing, gray dress waving a lantern. Light shot every which way, coming through the railings. The rays were brilliant, piercing; much brighter than any normal lantern. It hurt to look at it.

Bob thought to wake his wife but decided against it. Instead, he stood transfixed as the ghost floated across the top of the Casablanca Inn and simply vanished before his eyes. As if someone had turned off an old black-and-white television, the ghost's light contracted to a dim dot hovering where the spirit had been, then finally went out. Bob stood there, stupefied. When he finally shook off his shock, he realized he was drenched in sweat and gripping the drapes with both hands. He went back to bed, saving the story to tell Irene in the morning. Always a sound sleeper, she never heard or saw a thing. The couple stayed one more night in the same room but never again witnessed the ghost folks in St. Augustine have taken to calling the Lady with the Lantern.

Like Bob and Luis, most who have witnessed the Lady with the Lantern see her as a spirit perched atop the Casablanca, lamp in hand, waving her silent, eerie warning. In most cases the light stays close to the old widow's walk, though some witnesses have seen, and even videotaped, the mysterious light rising hundreds of feet in the air.

Others have experienced the ghost up close. Guests at the Casablanca have reported seeing the gray lady's spectral figure haunting the narrow hallways of the inn. Others say they've seen her image standing behind them when they look in the Casablanca's guest-room mirrors. One recent guest swears she had items removed from her luggage and placed around the room by a ghostly female figure she never saw, but that showed up in photographs she took at the Casablanca during her vacation.

Indeed, Anna's lantern-wielding spirit has been seen so often by so many that today she's a central figure in St. Augustine's thriving ghost-tour business. The promise of a ghostly encounter with her is a featured amenity on the bill of fare at the Casablanca Inn. But while everyone here knows the story of the heartbroken widow who continues to signal her long-lost outlaw lover, the storytellers never reveal her last name. Even her first name remains a matter of much debate. The tradition, locals say, grew from the desire to keep from slandering Anna's family, which remains very much a part of St. Augustine high society.

And so she gets to keep her good name. Cold comfort for an eternity spent trying to signal a true love known so briefly and lost forever to greed, vice, and an unforgiving sea. Watch for the light, always. Follow the light.

Chapter 2
Thomas Rowe's
Leading Lady

There's a dapper gentleman strolling the sands of St. Pete, look-
ing to welcome all comers to his luxurious seaside castle. When
he fades into the mist, it becomes clear his hospitality has survived
well beyond his death. And so has his love for a Spanish beauty.

The newlyweds strolled slowly, hand in hand, in the
sugar-white sand of St. Pete Beach. The sun was sinking
into the Gulf of Mexico and the new bride thought there
couldn't be a more perfectly romantic spot on earth. The
couple stopped to take in the view. She turned to her
new husband to kiss him and was startled by the sight of
a lone figure moving briskly up the beach behind them.
It was a man. In the fiery light of the tropical sunset, he
seemed to be glowing. He was dressed from head to toe
in white, from his Panama hat to his linen summer suit
and polished white bucks. He seemed strangely out of
place here on the beach. But even from this distance the
young woman could see he was smiling. The sight of him,
while unusual and unexpected, filled her with a feeling of
peace. Did he just tip his hat to her? She tugged on her
husband's arm.

"Honey, look. Look at this strange guy coming this
way."

Her husband turned to follow her gaze and saw . . .
nothing.

"What guy?"

The young wife was aghast. The friendly-looking man resplendent in his white summer finery had vanished right before her eyes. Where he'd stood, there was nothing but sand and shells.

"He was right there!" she shouted. "He looked like Panama Jack, and now he's just . . . gone!"

"It's hot out here," her husband said. "We've been out in the sun all day. We should head back to the hotel."

She pouted.

"I saw him. I really saw someone."

"I know you did, my dear," he said, absently kissing her sunburned forehead. "I'm sure you did."

The couple trekked back to their hotel, which rose like a giant pink sand castle from just above the high-water mark of St. Pete Beach. The Moorish towers of the Don CeSar hotel cast long shadows in the waning daylight. As they walked through the lobby, the woman pulled her husband over to the front desk. He cringed as she called the clerk over and launched into a detailed explanation of what she claimed she'd seen on the beach.

"All in white, crisp Panama hat," she told the clerk. "And then he just disappeared."

"Yes, ma'am," the Don CeSar employee replied. He was polite but decidedly unexcited. "I believe you saw Mr. Rowe. One of the greatest hoteliers in Florida history, I may add. He built the Don CeSar just as you see her now, and he is a common sight around the property."

"Well, I don't know why, but he seemed so friendly, even though he disappeared before we could meet," the woman said. "Would it be possible to make an appointment with Mr. Rowe and speak to him?"

"Oh, no, ma'am. I'm afraid not. This hotel was built in 1925. Thomas Rowe himself died in 1940. I'm afraid you're about fifty years too late to have a chat with our Mr. Rowe."

"So you're saying that was . . . what I saw out there, he was . . ."

"Yes, ma'am. Thomas Rowe's ghost."

"But why us?" the shaken young woman asked the unflappable desk clerk. "Why would he be coming toward us?"

"I imagine he wanted to make sure everything was to your liking," the clerk said.

"Really?"

"Sure. Oh, and also because you are in love. Mr. Rowe cannot resist true love."

Thomas Rowe's early life was far from a fairy-tale romance. Born in 1872 in a hardscrabble industrial town in Massachusetts, he was orphaned at the age of five and sent to rural England to be raised by his grandfather. He grew to be a whip-smart, strapping young lad who eventually made his way to London, where he enrolled in college and immersed himself in the arts and theater.

Before long, Thomas was a regular in London's opera houses. The performances, with their glorious costumes, amazing scenery, and brilliant music, captivated him. In the spring of 1892, some friends coaxed Tom into going to see a new production of *Maritana*. The light opera, written by Irishman William Vincent Wallace, had been wildly popular for decades in England. It wasn't unusual to hear folks singing songs from *Maritana* on the street.

"Do we need to see this old saw again?" Tom asked his friends. "Is there nothing more challenging for us to spend our time and precious coin on?"

"But this is the new *Maritana*," one of Thomas's friends urged. "This new cast of Spaniards is getting raves. Indulge us this once."

Thomas conceded and the group made its way to the theater. As the opera began, the crowd settled in to enjoy the show; all except Tom, who seemed bored and distracted, shifting in his seat and fidgeting through the overture. Then the curtain came up and she appeared. All at once it was as though Thomas Rowe's world had stopped short. There was no sound, no cast, no orchestra, no crowd. There was just her. A stunning Spanish beauty with dark hair and darker eyes. When she began to sing, her voice was angelic. Here, in a loge-level seat at an opera he'd been reluctant to attend, Thomas fell helplessly, hopelessly in love.

"Who is that?" he whispered to one of his friends.

"Who? The girl playing Maritana? That's Lucinda, one of the new Spanish cast. Isn't she fabulous?"

"Fabulous," Tom murmured, turning his gaze back to the stage. "Fabulous indeed."

He sat rapt for the remainder of the performance. When the curtain came down, his friends milled about getting ready to leave. But Tom wasted no time at all. He rushed to the door at the back of the theater and waited for this beautiful young heroine. After what seemed an eternity, she came out of the theater's rear stage door and into the cool London night. She was still in the guise of Maritana, the gypsy girl, her long brunette curls falling about her naked shoulders. In the gaslight of the city street she was even more radiant than she'd been on stage.

Tom approached her with feigned confidence. "I'm Thomas Rowe from America. I greatly enjoyed your performance tonight."

"I'm pleased to meet you, Thomas Rowe from America." Her English was perfect, tinged with just a hint of a highborn Spanish accent. "I am Lucinda. Would you walk me to the cast quarters?"

With that, she took his arm and the two walked the short distance to where she and the Spanish troupe were housed. They said nothing. But something powerful passed between them, because from that moment the dashing Thomas Rowe and the sultry Lucinda were inexorably connected. Tom attended nearly every performance of *Maritana*. And after a short time, he professed his love for Lucinda and she for him. Every moment available to them was spent in moonlight meetings in a little-known English courtyard, where Lucinda played Maritana and Rowe became the opera's hero, Don CeSar. The couple stood against the courtyard's fountain and re-created Maritana's love story in their own words.

Their love remained a secret, however, a forbidden thing. Lucinda's parents were Spanish aristocrats. Their plans for their daughter's future focused on culture and a career in the world of opera. She would tour internationally. She would be famous, rich, and adored by millions. Their plans certainly had no room for an American expatriate from a commoner's background, no matter how deep his infatuation for the beautiful young woman. The disapproval of Lucinda's parents was not enough to quell their clandestine meetings, however. With the rushing sound of the fountain as their musical score, they called each other Maritana and Don CeSar and made plans to run away together when

Lucinda's London performances were done. He promised her a pink castle of her own and a life of love and happiness.

The night before the final performance of *Maritana,* the two met in the courtyard they now called their "secret garden."

"I will be here tomorrow night, my love," Thomas told her. "I've hired a carriage and driver to take us to Southampton and booked passage on the next ship to America. When the final act is done, our first act begins. Meet me here and we'll away."

"I will be here, my Don CeSar," Lucinda said. "Nothing can keep us apart. There is nothing so strong as our love."

The following evening, Tom grinned as he passed the bustling crowd outside the theater. He skipped the performance and went directly to the tiny courtyard to await Lucinda. And there he waited. Hours passed. The carriage and driver waited impatiently outside the courtyard. And as the evening wore on and night turned to dawn, a dejected Thomas Rowe realized his love would not be coming. Tom paid the driver his promised fare and dismissed him, then the dejected young man made the long walk home. Alone.

The next day, friends who had attended the closing performance gave him the bad news. Lucinda's parents, suspicious that something was up between the young lovers, were waiting for her in the wings. They spirited her back to their country house in Spain and forbade her from contacting her American beau. Tom was heartbroken. He wrote to Lucinda constantly, but all of his letters were returned unopened. Lucinda's parents and their servants intercepted every letter and thwarted every attempt Tom made to reach out to his one true love. After several years of fruitless efforts, Thomas left London and returned to New England, where he threw himself into business and real estate development as a way to distract himself from his heartbreak.

He was, by most accounts, a success, but all who were close to him knew there was a hole in Tom's heart that could never really be filled. That hole widened considerably in 1902, when Tom opened a simple-looking letter postmarked from London. It was Lucinda's obituary. She'd taken ill shortly after they'd parted and never fully recovered. And now she was gone. She would never be his, at least not in this life. Attached to the obituary was a handwritten note from Lucinda, included by her father in response to her dying wish. It read:

Tom, My beloved Don CeSar.

Father promised me he would deliver you my message. Forgive them both as I have. Never would I despair. Nor could I forsake you. We found each other before and we shall do so again. This life is only an intermediate. I leave it without regret and travel to a place where the swing of the pendulum does not bring pain. Time is infinite. I will wait for you by our fountain to share our timeless love, our destiny is time.

Forever, Maritana.

Tom laid his head on the massive mahogany desk and wept bitterly.

From that day, Tom's robust health began to fail him. Tom's doctor, feeling the cold, Northeastern weather was wearing his patient down, suggested the tropical climate of Florida.

"It'll be good for you, Tom. Get away from the drab, depressing winters. Give you a new, sunny perspective on life. It's what you need."

Grudgingly, Tom heeded the advice. He could be miserable and lonely in the South as well as anywhere else, he figured.

In 1925 Thomas Rowe found St. Petersburg and began building a monument to his beloved Maritana. The Don CeSar was to be modeled after the Royal Hawaiian on Oahu and would be the Pink Palace he'd promised to Lucinda years before. It was a massive undertaking, the first hotel built on a Florida Gulf Coast beach. He laid down $100,000 for eighty acres on St. Petersburg's Long Key. The three hundred–room hotel cost him $1.5 million to build, not including the special pink paint he commissioned from DuPont for the exterior.

In the lobby, Tom painstakingly reconstructed the "secret garden." Every detail of the cobblestone courtyard and the fountain that bore witness to his love for Lucinda was re-created in the hotel.

The huge project had an obvious positive effect on Tom's health. He took to the role of tropical host, donning his signature white outfit and hat and attending to the needs of his growing clientele. By 1928, tourists were flocking to the world-class hotel, known by regulars as "The Don." An effusive host, Tom also became known as an equally gracious employer. He might never find true love again in this life, but he did get great satisfaction in making sure everyone around him was enjoying themselves.

The first indication that Tom and Lucinda's love transcended the mortal plane came in 1929, just before the stock market crash that presaged the Great Depression. Late one night, Tom awoke from a fitful sleep and felt the presence of his beloved Maritana. He never saw her, but he heard her voice whispering to him in the dark.

"Be ready, my love," the voice whispered. "You can weather the storm if you prepare now."

Based on the supernatural warning, Thomas squirreled away cash in secret vaults throughout the Don CeSar. The money sustained him and his staff during the worst of the financial turmoil of the 1930s. Re-energized, The Don played host to countless celebrities. F. Scott Fitzgerald, Lou Gehrig, Ernest Hemingway, and Al Capone all signed the guest register at the Don CeSar. Tom never stopped brainstorming for ideas for his Pink Palace. With business slow in March and April, he called his friends in New York and invited the Yankees baseball team to stay and train at the Don CeSar, making the team the first to engage in spring training in Florida.

By 1940, Tom's health was failing again. He moved from his penthouse suite to Room 101, right behind the reception desk. In the fall of that year, on a balmy afternoon, Thomas Rowe walked into the lobby of his hotel and stood beside his beloved fountain. He gripped his chest and fell to his knees. Employees rushed to his aid and helped him to his room. Bystanders swear they saw a wave of light in the shape of a young woman sweep into the hotel and follow the stricken man to his chamber. Within minutes, Tom was dead of a heart attack. The light hovered outside his room briefly, then returned to the fountain before disappearing completely.

Since Thomas Rowe's death, the Don CeSar has been through good times and bad. In 1942, the U.S. Army purchased the Pink Palace and the Don CeSar became a convalescent hospital for World War II pilots. Years passed and eventually the government had no more use for the property. The Don became a derelict with boarded-up windows and barricaded doors. During the days the Pink Palace stood as an abandoned and dilapidated hulk, stories started cropping up of lights shining through boarded windows. The place was scheduled for demolition in 1972, but a St. Petersburg historical group rescued The Don from the wrecking ball and secured a multimillion-dollar grant for restoration. Even during the rehabilitation, Tom couldn't stay away from the place he called his own Taj Mahal, built for his long-lost love. Workers on the project were frequently approached by a friendly man in a white linen suit and a Panama hat. He asked them how things were progressing and gave them advice on certain repairs. And he always disappeared before anyone could ask who he was or how he had accessed the secured construction site.

By 1975, the Don CeSar was once again open for business. But the return of business at The Don also brought about a resurgence of mysterious, supernatural activity in the place. When a housekeeping staffer was cleaning the fifth floor, where Thomas Rowe once lived, she repeatedly heard knocking on the door of the room she was cleaning. After becoming irritated when she opened the door and no one was there, she went downstairs and found that all the other housekeepers were already gone for the day. No one else had been assigned to the fifth floor. Until the day she retired, the housekeeper refused to clean any room on that dreaded floor.

One morning when dawn arrived and the sun began streaming through the eastern windows, the morning desk clerk found a guest asleep in a lobby chair. When the staffer approached, the guest awoke with a start.

"I was asleep and the shower just suddenly came on," the guest said. "I turned it off and went back to bed. Then the bathroom door started opening and closing. I got dressed and came down here. I'm not sleeping in any room with a ghost."

When a veteran reservation clerk made her way down to the kitchen for a tray of cups and a pot of tea, she was shocked when upon her return, the swinging doors opened before her approach. This incident was apparently repeated and was even witnessed on more than one occasion. Perhaps Thomas Rowe was portraying the hotelier and gentleman he was in life, and helping another of his staff members.

After the Don CeSar became listed on the National Trust for Historic Hotels in America, new ghost stories started circulating. Though smoking has long been banned in much of the hotel, workers and guests report the strong odor of menthol cigarettes. Tom smoked them until the day he died, on the advice of his doctor, who thought cigarettes would soothe Tom's persistent asthma.

One former executive came within a locked door from interrupting Tom and Lucinda in an intimate moment. As he approached his ground-floor office on the south side of the Don CeSar, he clearly heard the voices of a man and a woman engaged in the kind of low banter unique to lovers. He froze in place, unsure whether to proceed, or to run. After all, he had the only key to this locked office. He turned the lock and the lovers' patter ceased. He heard the couple get up and leave the room, even though there are no other doors. He even heard the rustle of Lucinda's skirt as she rose to depart.

Not only is the ghost of Thomas Rowe helpful to satisfied guests, but he can be abrupt with those who criticize The Don, as well. Once, when a customer spoke harshly of the hotel's service to an employee in the hotel floral shop, all of the flowers in the cooler suddenly wilted in unison. Another woman who was nitpicking the hotel's culinary offerings found her skirt being pulled up and away from her. Only when she froze and stopped complaining did her garment fall back into place.

Then there are the most persistent supernatural sightings: the visions of a young couple strolling the grounds and the fifth floor hand in hand at sunset, the man always wearing the traditional tropical-weather white suit and Panama hat, the young, beautiful woman with the long, dark hair wearing a Spanish-style peasant dress. Those who believe say it's clear that Lucinda and Tom finally made a life together in the Pink Palace he built as her tribute. Free from overprotective parents and a world that forbade their love, the couple are now free to roam Don CeSar's marble halls and manicured grounds together, sharing the Afterlife.

Chapter 3
The
Lovesick Nurse

The young girl couldn't save the man she adored in her lifetime. But her spirit keeps vigil at this old Virginia boarding school where North and South met in battle, and in love.

The rest of the girls were busily packing their things, rushing to catch one final coach out of Abingdon. The once-quiet corner of the Blue Ridge Highlands in southwest Virginia was now on the front lines of the Civil War, and the Martha Washington Girls School was no longer a safe place for the few teens left there. Besides, Confederate soldiers and doctors had taken over the building and turned it into a field hospital for a growing number of war wounded. And so they gathered what they could carry and prepared for a long ride home. All except Beth.

Beth had decided to stay at Martha Washington; after all, she'd come to the private boarding school in hopes of becoming a nurse. Now she had a chance to help the war effort and experience nursing firsthand. Though she was barely fourteen years old, the doctors said they'd be glad to have her. As she waved goodbye to her schoolmates in the winter of 1861, Beth Anne Smith became the youngest nurse at Martha Washington.

"You're certain about this, are you?" one of the senior nurses asked Beth.

"I am. Very much so." Beth had a stubborn streak, but she was also quite talented. She was top of her class in science and math. And she was a skilled violinist, pianist, and singer. She had every intention of using all of her skills to impress the staff and help her new patients.

Beth set about the ordinary tasks of the nurse trainee, changing dressings, cleaning wounds, and helping to move patients from room to room. She also made time to sing to them or play her violin, hoping the music would give the wounded men some comfort. Most were in too much pain, or too bitter and hardened from the gory battles they'd endured to get much pleasure from the young girl's music, but still she persisted.

"Shall I play for you?" she would ask a new patient politely. And if no answer was forthcoming, she'd take it as a yes and sweetly serenade them for as long as she could.

The staff loved the tender, genuine concern Beth showed for the patients, and most of them loved her music. Occasionally, however, she had to be told to stop playing in order to carry out some routine hospital task. Such was the case on the morning of April 11, 1861. Beth was playing her violin and singing quietly in a ward of wounded men when she was interrupted.

"Beth. A moment please."

She abruptly stopped playing and ran to face the doctor who'd summoned her.

"Yes, sir. I was just . . ."

"I know, my dear. I know. The music is lovely, but let's give the men some rest for a moment, shall we? The water in the kitchen is nearly drained. Go down to the well and fetch some more, would you please? That's a good girl."

"I will, sir," Beth said. "Right away."

She put away her instrument and grabbed two pails from the kitchen pantry.

"I'm headed to the well!" she shouted to the nurses in the hallway.

"Be careful out there!" one of them yelled back. "I thought I heard shooting from over the ridge!"

Beth was too busy running out the door to hear their warning. As much as she loved working in the hospital, she really enjoyed getting outside, feeling the wind on her face, smelling the pine and the early spring flowers. She got to be a child again, if just for a while, as she ran full speed down the road, the metal pails clanging in her tiny hands.

She skipped along Plum Alley, a quaint misnomer for a road named because it cut plumb through the village of Abingdon. When she got to the well at Valley Street, she immediately sensed something was wrong. There was an eerie silence. No birds, no crickets, no sound at all. Beth froze. Suddenly, her whole world erupted in a thundering barrage of bullets and hoofbeats and shouts and screaming. Beth jumped into a thicket and hid as a Yankee soldier on horseback raced around the corner and ground to a dusty stop just feet away from her hiding place. The young girl watched in horror as a squad of Confederate soldiers arrived in pursuit of the Union officer. The Yankee got off one shot before he and his horse were met with a hail of Confederate gunfire. The bluecoat fell, and his horse toppled on top of him. Mortally wounded and being crushed by the bleeding animal, the soldier cried out.

"Help me. Help. Someone please help me."

Beth was so close she could see into the Yankee soldier's eyes. She was frozen with fear. The Confederates, convinced they'd dispatched their enemy, who now lay under his mount, turned back on Valley Street to rejoin their company. Though she was haunted by the cries of the wounded man lying right in front of her, fear got the best of young Beth. She ran from the bushes and sprinted back to the Martha Washington, leaving her water pails behind.

When she got back to the makeshift hospital, she was nearly incoherent.

A doctor grabbed the girl by her shoulders. "Beth, what is it? What's wrong, girl?"

"A man, a soldier, a Yankee soldier has been shot. He was crying out. He's dying . . ." Beth trailed off into tears at the thought of the wounded trooper and how she'd left him behind when he needed help.

"You did the right thing, Beth," the doctor said. "Getting yourself killed wouldn't help anyone.

"That area will be too dangerous while the fighting is still going on," he said. "The best we can do is wait until nightfall and try to get to him then. Now go get some rest, dear. You've had an awful fright."

Beth tried to calm down, but all she could think about was the poor soldier and those eyes. Hurt, pleading, she couldn't shake the thought of it.

When night finally came, Beth led a small group of doctors and nurses to the place where she'd seen the soldier felled. The group approached carefully, worried that Confederate soldiers might still be patrolling the area and mistake them for the enemy. That they were out in the dark helping a Union officer probably wouldn't have gone over well with the rebel troops either. Miraculously, as they approached the downed horse, they found the wounded man trapped, but still alive.

"Please. Please help me," he said weakly.

As they pulled him free and loaded him onto a small cart, Beth tried her best to clean the caked dirt and blood from his face.

"Who are you?" she asked innocently.

"I am Captain John Stoves," the soldier said. "And you are my angel."

With that, Stoves fell unconscious.

The cadre of doctors and nurses pulled the wounded twenty-year-old back to the hospital and through a private rear entrance, for fear of attracting the attention of the rebel soldiers stationed around the Martha Washington. Stoves was laid in Preston Parlor, the large dorm room Beth had once shared with her schoolmates. Those school days seemed like years ago. She was a war nurse now. Beth insisted on sitting by John Stoves's side through the night, holding his hand and dabbing at his forehead with a wet cloth to keep his fever down.

Standing in the Preston Parlor doorway, one of the nurses whispered to her senior colleague.

"Look at her. She's falling in love with this one."

"You're too late," the older nurse replied. "She fell for him as soon as she saw him hit the ground."

For the next three days Beth kept a constant vigil at the bedside of Captain Stoves. The rest of the hospital, meanwhile, was overrun with casualties from the same Valley Street battle Beth had witnessed. Twenty-seven wounded soldiers were brought to the Martha Washington on April 12. Nine died. But Beth ignored all of it. She sat by Captain Stoves's bedside playing her violin and singing. She felt herself falling in love with the Yankee.

On the morning of April 14, Stoves went into convulsions. He was bleeding into his lungs; he was drowning in his hospital bed.

"Play something, Beth," Stoves sputtered. "Please play something for me. I'm going."

Beth ran from the room to get help. A team of doctors and nurses followed the frantic young girl to Stoves's bedside. Beth cradled the soldier in her tiny arms and the doctors checked over the mortally wounded man.

"He's unconscious, Beth. He's dying," one doctor told her.

"He's alive, he is alive!" she screamed. She stroked his hair and sang to him as the doctors performed chest compressions. The internal damage was too great, however. Stoves shook violently one last time and opened his eyes, a trickle of blood running from the corner of his mouth.

"Beth, my pain, my pain . . . my pain is gone." He slipped away with a peaceful smile on his face.

"No, he isn't. Please don't let him die, please don't let him die," Beth cried. She covered his body with her own, refusing to let the doctors pull the sheet over his face. "Please, don't let him die, dear God."

Despite her protests, Captain John Stoves was dead. Beth continued to weep over her young soldier well into the morning. Around 1 a.m. she was joined in her vigil by a few other hospital staff, who sat in the candlelit room and marveled at the depth of her emotion for a young soldier she barely knew. Suddenly a chill wind blew through the ward, extinguishing all of the candles in the room. In the pitch blackness, a light appeared at the foot of Stoves's bed. It grew into the shape of a woman and hovered there in a misty, eerie silence.

"Who's there?" one of the doctors called out. "Who are you?"

The angel before them spoke.

"You did your best to comfort him. He's well taken care of now. Be joyful." With that, the spirit vanished and the room went dark.

The next morning, Beth played a sweet, haunting tune on her violin as the nurses prepared Stoves's body for burial. The solemn scene was interrupted when a Confederate soldier burst in, claiming he had orders from his commander to take Captain Stoves as a prisoner. Beth stood and approached the rebel soldier defiantly.

"Tell your commander Captain Stoves has been pardoned by an officer higher than General Lee," the young girl said. "Captain Stoves is dead."

Beth Anne Smith spent the next year in quiet mourning in the hospital at the Martha Washington. She cared for the sick and was a highly regarded young nurse, though she never got over the death of her Yankee soldier. In April 1862, a year after the death of Captain John Stoves, Beth was making her way down the stairs to the Martha Washington chapel when she collapsed. She was taken to a bed in Preston Parlor, the same room where she'd cared for Captain Stoves. Doctors were summoned to check on her. She was diagnosed with scarlet fever. On April 14—exactly one year after Stoves died—Beth succumbed to the disease. Though she was much too weak to speak, she asked the nurses for paper and pencil. She scribbled a note in shaky hand.

"Please pray for me and please bury me next to Captain John Stoves."

They kept her wishes. Both Captain Stoves and Beth Anne Smith were buried in the nearby Abingdon Cemetery. Perhaps the young girl thought she could join Captain Stoves in death, even if she could not be with him in life. It did not work.

✝

Built first as a private residence in 1830 and converted to a school in 1854, the old Martha Washington building has, in the 140-plus years since Beth's death, gone from wartime hospital to military barracks to boardinghouse for local actors. In 1935, the historic Georgian-style brick building was turned into a fifty-one-room inn complete with spa and saltwater pool. It's in this incarnation that Beth has made her presence known—along with her undying and unrequited love for Captain Stoves.

Guests at the Martha Washington regularly see the figure of a young girl ascending the stairs of the inn wearing the telltale purple apron dress common to Civil War nurses. She also wears the same high-buckle shoes, caked with red-clay mud, that she wore on the fateful day she saw her dear soldier ambushed. Even when she is not seen, she can be heard. Violin music is frequently heard drifting down the corridors in the early morning, though the source of the sound can never be discovered.

One guest several years ago saw the young nurse looking forlorn at the base of the main stairway. When he approached and asked if he could help her, the spirit dissolved into a cloud that evaporated as he watched in horror.

As frightening as some of the encounters are, most of those who run across Beth's restless spirit say the prevailing sense is one of quiet sadness. From the moment she hid in the bushes on that fateful day on Valley Street, all Beth Anne Smith ever wanted to do was help and comfort her one true love. At the Martha Washington, she's spending eternity still trying to deliver that loving care.

Chapter 4

Emily's
Bridge

The old wooden covered bridge is quintessential New England. But the ferocious female ghost who haunts this Vermont landmark gives regular testimony to the transcendent fury of a jilted lover.

The four teenagers had driven out here looking for trouble. They found it. Their headlights barely pierced the blackness inside the narrow, one-lane covered wooden bridge. It was clear, however, that they were not alone in this remote section of Vermont. Floating midway across the bridge was a brilliantly glowing, translucent figure of a woman. She was facing away from the terrified teens. But not for long.

As the ghostly woman turned toward the intruders, they saw her face contorted with pain and rage, her eyes wild. Even with the windows of their car rolled up tight against the cold, dark Vermont night, they could hear her low shriek rising in volume and pitch as she flew at them with violent intent. The kids scrambled to lock their doors. The specter circled their car several times, grabbing the door handles and shaking the whole vehicle with otherworldly force. The driver threw the car into reverse and gunned the engine, tires spitting gravel and dust as he fishtailed back toward the main road that had led them from downtown Stowe to this hellish encounter. The ghost stayed right with the careening car briefly, but as they backed around a turn and the bridge faded from sight, the ghoul stopped short. The chilling sound of tearing sheet metal filled the car, but the driver kept his foot on the gas until the group was a safe distance from the bridge and under the comforting glow of one of the area's rare street lamps.

"What was that?!" one of the girls in the backseat shouted. The entire group was near hysterics.

"You know what that was!" one of the boys screamed. "That was Emily. You wanted to see her—well, you saw her. Now let's get out of here!"

Before they left, the driver got out and cautiously peeked around the back side of the car. There, all across the rear quarter of the car just above the tire, four deep gouges had torn clear through the metal body.

"She tried to kill us," was all he could say when he slid back behind the wheel. "She really tried to kill us."

Those four teens who ventured out to the Gold Brook Bridge on an ill-advised dare one winter night joined a long list of folks around Stowe, Vermont, who vow to never again get near the place. The picture-postcard beauty of the quaint, historic covered bridge conceals an ugly truth. The Gold Brook Bridge is really Emily's Bridge. It's home to one especially mean-spirited ghost who took up eternal residence in the antique structure after she lost the one and only love of her life. Emily wasn't always a shrieking she-demon, of course. It took a fair bit of heartbreak and betrayal to turn her into one.

Emily was born in Stowe in 1829 to deeply religious parents. She was a shy girl, awkward and overweight, but kind and intelligent. She'd walk the roads between Stowe's three villages, marveling at the natural beauty of the Vermont countryside. She loved children and animals and Vermont's brilliant autumn colors. All she wanted was someone who understood her and loved her for who she was. By the time she was nineteen, however, she began to think that sort of person might never come along. She watched other women around Stowe, some of them in her own family, growing older year after year all by themselves. It seemed such a sad, hopeless future. Not her future, she prayed.

Though the prospect of being alone frightened Emily, it certainly didn't bother her parents. Her father was a harsh man who suffered little of Emily's fanciful talk about beauty and nature and, above all, love and marriage. Her place was at home, helping her quiet, obedient mother with the household chores and saying her prayers for several hours every evening, he said.

It was not at all the life Emily pined for.

So when Donald, the son of a local furniture maker, began taking an interest in Emily in the spring of 1849, she was nearly overwhelmed with giddy excitement. Donald wasn't even remotely handsome. His family was poor even by rustic Vermont standards. Still, she imagined herself as his wife, sharing their days together with a cozy house and children of their own.

At twenty-one years old, Donald wasn't any more familiar with love and relationships than Emily. He spent most of his free time working in his father's shop. A gawky teen who'd grown into an even gawkier young man, he'd never courted a girl or even held hands until the day Emily reached out and took his varnish-stained hand in hers. When she did, he was hooked.

Their romance blossomed quickly, this awkward, unlikely pair. Emily stole away every moment she could to meet

Donald, who had taken to spending less and less time in the furniture shop and more time with the young woman who adored him and hung on his every word. Their favorite meeting spot became the new wooden bridge that local builder John W. Smith had constructed across Gold Brook. It was both a romantic and a practical choice. Here they could meet a fair distance from the nearest house, surrounded by the singing birds, fragrant flowers, and gently rushing waters. Since the bridge linked Stowe's villages, Emily could walk from her home in Center Village and meet Donald when he ducked out of his shop and ran past the sawmill in Moscow. They shared their first kiss in the shadow of the bridge. And Donald stammered and stuttered through his first "I love you" as they strolled across the sturdy span.

Within a few months, the young couple decided to share their secret romance with the world. They wanted to be married. Despite a lifetime of being told to forsake thoughts of boys and love in favor of God and family, Emily was sure her parents would be thrilled about her engagement. She was wrong. Emily's father was furious when he heard that his daughter had been secretly meeting a man, the son of a common tradesman, no less.

"His father is unskilled at his craft and his good-for-nothing son is less so," bellowed her father. "I forbid it. You shall not see him again."

"But Father . . ."

"No! Go to your room and pray for forgiveness. For you to even think about such things is shameful."

Emily looked to her mother for help, but the old woman stayed focused on her sewing. There was nowhere to turn. Emily's family was denying her one chance to be happy; the one chance she thought might never come. Now it was here, but it was being taken away. Emily vowed to herself in that moment that she would defy her parents. She loved Donald and he loved her. They would be married no matter what her father said.

"Very well," Emily said, going quietly to her room.

"I will miss you both," she added quietly when she was out of earshot.

The next day, Donald and Emily met at the bridge as planned. Emily ran to her lover and embraced him.

"What did your father say?" Donald asked anxiously.

"What does it matter?" Emily replied, her head against his chest. "I love you. Oh, Donald. Let's just run away together. Just the two of us. That's all we need. Just us."

"So your father said no, then?"

"I love you, Donald. Just say you'll always be with me."

"I will, Emily. I will."

The young couple crawled to their favorite secret spot on the banks of Gold Brook directly beneath the bridge where they could not be seen. Normally, they'd spend their afternoons here stealing kisses and expressing their love, but today was different. They started planning their escape from Stowe and from Emily's parents. It was decided there, under the Gold Brook Bridge, that after sundown on the evening after next, Donald and Emily would meet in that very spot with whatever they could carry and head off to start their new life together. Their plan was a simple one. Too simple.

Emily's father, anticipating that his daughter was planning to disobey him, made an unannounced visit to the furniture builder's shop in Moscow the next morning. Donald watched in mute terror as the man approached his father and asked to have a word with him. Emily's father then turned to Donald.

"Leave us, boy."

Donald scampered away like a kicked cur. He stood outside the shop trying to listen. What he heard made his heart sink. Emily's father, a powerful businessman in Stowe, was threatening the furniture maker. If his son ever went near Emily again, the old man swore he'd make certain the furniture shop was ruined. Nobody within five hundred miles would ever buy anything turned out of the shop again unless Donald gave up Emily forever. The boy was crushed. When Emily's father left, Donald went back into the shop and saw his own father weeping silently.

"You must do what is in your heart, son," his father told him.

"I will, Father. I'll do what's in my heart."

Two nights hence, with the sun fully set, Emily's heart was racing with fear and anticipation. She'd taken a bedsheet and tied it into a sack to pack some clothing and a few precious things she wanted to take with her. Mother and Father were settled in near the fire for their evening prayers. They would come looking for her soon. She had to leave. Now.

Lugging her belongings over one shoulder, Emily slipped quietly out the back door and into the brisk New England night. The stars were brilliant overhead and the full frost moon bathed the countryside in bright blues and grays. She walked slowly along the dirt road, scuffing through the small stones, breathing in the night air, trying one last time to savor the pleasures of the only world she'd ever known. She had no idea where she'd be tomorrow. But she was sure she'd be with her Donald.

When Emily arrived at Gold Brook Bridge she was surprised to find herself alone. She'd hoped Donald would be waiting for her. She wanted to run into his arms. Perhaps he'd been delayed by his father. Maybe he was having trouble carrying his things up from Moscow Village. Emily didn't mind. She sat and listened to the call of a screech owl and stared at the sky. An hour went by. Cold and increasingly worried, Emily set her bag down on a dry spot and began to pace around the opening of the bridge. Where was he? What was happening? She wondered if maybe he'd gone under the bridge. Maybe he'd fallen and was hurt. Her mind raced.

In the stark, flat moonlight, Emily picked her way down the bank to their secret spot under the bridge. Tacked to a stump there was a ragged piece of birch bark. Emily felt her head swimming. What was this? What was happening? She grabbed the bark and brought it back out from under the bridge, out into the moonlight where she could see it. In a rough hand, a message had been scratched with a flint:

"Emily, I'm sorry. It cannot be. Our fathers say so. Love, Donald."

Emily scrambled the rest of the way up the bank and stood at the mouth of the bridge. She turned the note over and over in her hands. It cannot be? Sorry? Love, Donald? A rage like nothing she'd ever felt in her young life swept over her. From her very core she screamed her loudest, a shriek so piercing it echoed around the hills of Stowe for several minutes even after she'd been reduced to quiet sobbing. Heartbroken, she went to her bag that held the few remaining things she'd cared about. She untied the knot and the top of the sheet and dumped her belongings down the embankment and into the brook. A china doll and several delicate glass animals shattered on the rocks below.

She shook the sheet empty, then carried it into the suffocating black of the covered bridge. Climbing up the rail, she shimmied her way along one rafter to the massive center beam that supported the bridge's room. Her feet dangled fifteen feet above the bridge deck as she looped the bedsheet over the beam and tied it off with a double knot. She looped the free end around her neck and tied it as tight as she could. Nobody would be able to cross the bridge without finding her, she thought. With no further pause, without a second thought, she pushed herself off the rafter. The sheet jerked tight with a sickening snap. Emily's body swung in the night air in the center of the Gold Brook Bridge. The heartsick teen chose death over a life without her love.

Donald continued unremarkably in his father's business and was quickly forgotten. Emily, however, has been burned into Stowe's collective memory for 160 years. Stories of her lost love and horrific end were common in the years following her death. But it was only after the death of her parents decades later that townspeople began to report spectacular and frightening encounters with the aggressive ghost that haunts what came to be known as Emily's Bridge.

Horses would often refuse to cross the bridge. When coaxed, the animals were sometimes subjected to mysterious clawlike scratches as they passed the middle of the span.

Pedestrians heard a woman wailing and crying from some-where inside—or under—the bridge. But it was the visions at night that convinced folks around Stowe that Emily's spirit was not content to go quietly into the Afterlife.

Even after the bridge was declared a historic monument and painstakingly restored in 1969, the place remained bet-ter known as Emily's haunt than as a quaint Vermont arti-fact. Her spirit is especially agitated by teen thrill seekers and young lovers who seek out the romantic tranquility of Gold Brook.

In November 2002, freelance writer Dennis Rousseau was passing through Stowe on assignment for a travel maga-zine. He stopped at a trading post in the Center Village. His instincts told him this would be a good place to get tips on what to see.

"Afternoon," the elderly store clerk said.

"Hi there," Dennis said. "I'm looking for a good cup of coffee, and maybe directions to the prettiest place in town."

"Ayuh," the clerk said dryly. "I guess you could get both here."

"Cream and sugar," Dennis said.

Coffee in hand, Dennis pulled up a rickety stool and chatted up the old man, telling him about his magazine assignment and asking what there was to see in Stowe. The store clerk rattled off the usual list of attractions. The old inns, the downtown theater, the Congregational church. He paused awhile before getting to the last one.

"Lot of folks like to go up the old Gold Brook Bridge," he said. "Then again, lots of folks don't."

"What's there?" Dennis asked, intrigued.

"Lovely old bridge, and one angry young woman."

"Property owner? Look, sir, I don't want to be trespassing on anyone's land here."

"Oh no, boy. She doesn't own the place. She just thinks she does."

The old man gave Dennis a short version of Emily's story. It sounded to the young reporter like the perfect kind of place, the perfect anecdote, to include in his story. The scenic beauty of Vermont stitched to a love story turned morbid horror tale. If he was lucky, maybe he'd even get to see a ghost.

Dennis was very lucky.

He followed the old man's directions and arrived at the bridge just as the afternoon sky began to melt from blue to red. He had gotten out of his rental car to take in the scene when he noticed a glow coming from the center of the darkened bridge. Despite a growing uneasiness, he felt himself drawn to the mysterious light. As he approached the black maw of the bridge, the glowing shape swung slowly from left to right. Suddenly, Dennis was met with a piercing scream. The glowing shape, now clearly the specter of a translucent woman, rushed at him, shrieking. He covered his head and closed his eyes and a cold wind blew over him, stirring up a choking cloud of dust. He waited until everything had gone quiet.

He stood and brushed himself off. All around him the Vermont dusk was quiet, normal, beautiful. He squinted into the dark covered bridge and saw something waving gently in the evening breeze. He took a few steps into the bridge, close enough to see a tattered bedsheet hanging from the bridge's center beam.

Chapter 5
Raynham's
Brown Lady

They could lock away the lady of the house for her supposed indiscretions, but they couldn't contain her spirit, which haunts the marble halls of this stately English manor to this day. Some say she's even posed for the camera!

This was exactly the distraction Frederick Marryat had been looking for. The past year had been a whirlwind of parties and praise and travel and success. Everywhere he traveled, his latest novel, *Mr. Midshipman Easy,* was the talk of the town. Here, back home in England, even close friends like Charles Dickens were heaping flattery on him. He'd come a long way, from decorated Royal Navy captain in the Napoleonic Wars to darling of Britain's literary circles. Was it possible, he wondered, that his contemporaries were right? Dickens was telling folks that Captain Frederick Marryat had invented the sea novel. It was all heady stuff.

So stealing away to a friend's estate in the English countryside in the spring of 1836 for a few days of adventure was a welcome break. Several other friends already lodged there had invited him to the retreat for a hunting and shooting party. That the visit also came with the possibility of encountering a ghost added to the allure. He'd always been adventurous to a fault, Marryat thought to himself. As he made his way up the impossibly grand staircase that formed the spine of Raynham Hall, he paused only briefly, wondering for a second whether maybe he wasn't pushing things a bit too far this time.

Nonsense, he thought. *We'll eat and drink and hunt and shoot. And if I have my wits scared out of me, perhaps I'll have the makings of my next book.*

"So this will be the actual room, then?" Marryat asked as he made his way up the steps.

"The actual room indeed," said his friend and host, the latest in a long line of Townshend family members to have occupied Raynham Hall in Norfolk, England, since it was built in 1619. "You'll be quartered in the chambers where Dorothy Townshend spent her final, miserable days and nights. You still game for this? We have plenty of other rooms here, you know."

Marryat stopped on the stairs a moment, shook off any doubt, and trudged upward and onward.

"Let's go," he said. "Let's meet your ghostly ancestor."

As the two men made their way upstairs, Marryat took in the splendor of the place. Approaching the outside of the grand building had been stunning, to be sure. Raynham Hall is a marvel of seventeenth-century Italian craftsmanship in an area otherwise dedicated to mostly Elizabethan buildings. Its massive, pillared stone front thrusts up from the Norfolk countryside like a defiant fist. But if the exterior was impressive, the interior of Raynham Hall was positively breathtaking. Marryat looked down across the black-and-white checkerboard floor of the estate's main Marble Hall and followed the ornate plasterwork up to the center of the ceiling above his head. There, a rearing doe and stag on either side of a crowned globe adorned the Townshend family crest.

The halls leading to Marryat's guest chamber were equally well appointed. Treasures befitting a titled British royal family were everywhere. Most impressive, Marryat thought, were the portraits—dark, somber faces in even darker frames—of the barons, viscounts, and marquesses that had called Raynham Hall their home for three centuries.

"Who is this?" Marryat asked his host. He pointed to a three-quarter-length portrait of a long-haired, round-faced gent in full royal robes, a half smirk on his thin lips. "He seems like a friendly sort."

"That's Turnip," Marryat's host replied. "The Lord Charles 2nd Viscount Townshend. One of the most famous men to ever grace these halls, a noted Member of Parliament, adviser to King George I."

"I'm sorry, did you say, 'Turnip'?"

"Yes. Turnip Townshend. The lord of the manor pioneered crop rotation for all of England through his agricultural experiments here at Raynham. A rather unfortunate nickname for such an important effort, don't you think? He's also the man responsible for much of the misery visited upon the dead woman you want so badly to meet. Strange what love will make people do, living or dead."

Marryat studied the painting up close. In it, Charles Townshend stood, one hand on his hip, the other resting on a plain, round table. Marryat thought the viscount looked like a no-nonsense guy, perhaps a little embarrassed by the trappings of his royalty; uncomfortable in the layer upon layer of velvet, silk, fur, and gold piping.

"So this is Dorothy's husband and one true love," Marryat said mostly to himself. "Have mercy."

"Too late for that, I'm afraid. Okay, this way to your room, my friend."

The door to Marryat's guest chamber was a massive hunk of dark, knotty oak noticeably less ornate than the other doors in that section of the house. As he made his way into the room, he noticed the door could be locked with thick, brass deadbolts from both inside and out. The chamber was comfortable, but not nearly as thoughtfully decorated as the rest of the estate. The lone piece of art in the room was a full-figure portrait of a delicate, dark-eyed beauty. Her porcelain skin glowed against the dark brown brocade of her dress. She was looking furtively over her left shoulder, her dainty right hand extended in the opposite direction as if keeping an eye out while beckoning some unseen stranger. A small metal plaque on the painting was engraved simply, "Dolly."

"This is Dorothy Townshend?" Marryat asked.

"The very same. The Brown Lady herself," came the reply.

"She is quite beautiful," the author said.

"Was. She *was* quite beautiful. Those who see her these days don't find her nearly so attractive, I'm afraid."

Marryat's host, himself a titled member of the Townshend family, regaled his guest with tales of the Brown Lady's frightening appearances. She liked to scare both family residents and guests by haunting the main stairway and the upstairs halls. And a visit from the ghost of Dolly Townshend was rarely a pleasant experience. Her specter had been described as brooding, angry, and confrontational. This young Lord Townshend told Marryat that many of the visions began in this very room, right in the vicinity of her own portrait. Sure, it looked like a normal painting by the light of day. But by the flicker of candlelight in the late evening, the image took on a sinister glow. Dolly's face would look drawn, skull-like, the eyes reduced to hollow dark orbs.

Marryat heard how, just six years before, King George IV had visited Raynham Hall to spend some quiet time while recovering from one of the many illnesses that plagued him.

His vacation at Raynham was hardly relaxing, however. In the middle of his first night there, the king awoke to find the glimmering female ghost standing at the foot of his bed. She glared at the monarch before disappearing through an open window. George IV rose, alerted his entourage, and left Raynham Hall in the dead of night, never to return.

"I will not spend another hour in this accursed house, for tonight I have seen that which I hope to God I never see again!" the king told his companions.

Hearing these stories, Marryat couldn't keep from staring at the painting now.

"What could have happened that hurt this woman so?" Marryat asked.

"She loved a Townshend, then lost that love, found it, and lost it again," was the reply. "More pain than one mortal lifetime could hope to contain, I imagine."

Dorothy Walpole was a fetching and high-born young woman of privilege at a time when such things, breeding and beauty, were matters of ultimate importance. By 1698, when she was barely thirteen years old, Dolly was stunning and mature beyond her years. She was also deeply in love, professing her undying adoration for a dashing young blueblood who did business with her family. She told her father, a powerful politician in the House of Commons, that the young viscount under his guardianship, Charles Townshend, was the man she wanted to marry.

Even without Dolly's romantic teenage inclinations, the pairing made sense. Dorothy Walpole was the daughter of a well-known legislator and the sister of an up-and-coming

Parliamentarian who would go on to become England's first prime minister. Joining the Walpoles of Norfolk's Houghton region with the Townshends of Raynham would create a regional political powerhouse. There was one problem, however.

The elder Walpole had been quarreling with the Lord Townshend. Walpole found his charge an intelligent and capable young man, but there was something about Charles that grated on him personally. He was opinionated, argumentative, crass. He wielded his birthright like a club and rarely suffered contradiction. Walpole liked the young man well enough, but he most certainly did not love him. Beyond that, there was the potential political backlash such a union would engender. Rivals would see the marriage as an attempt by Walpole to use his guardianship of Townshend for the benefit of his family. After brief contemplation, Walpole gave his daughter an answer. She could not marry Charles Townshend. In fact, she was forbidden from ever seeing him again.

The young girl was heartbroken. She cried and begged, to no avail. The decision had been made. Her love was not powerful enough to overcome her father's political will. Crushed, Dolly Walpole sank into a deep depression. Her fragile emotional state only got worse when, later that year, it was announced that Charles Townshend was to marry Elizabeth Pelham, daughter of Baron Pelham of Laughton. Lovesick, Dolly swore rebellion.

For the next decade she traveled Europe. To stem the heartbreak, and to punish her image-obsessed father, she drank, gambled, and engaged in a fair number of very public romances with men of various reputations and marital states. Her own reputation was in tatters by the time she returned to Norfolk and took up with a notorious womanizer and profligate named Lord Wharton. That might have been the end of any designs she had on being with the man she truly loved, except that tragedy was about to visit Raynham Hall.

In 1711, after the difficult birth of their fifth child, Elizabeth Pelham died, leaving Charles Townshend a most eligible widower. If she had been a beautiful girl, Dorothy Walpole at age twenty-five was even more alluring. After an appropriate mourning period, Dolly called on Charles and confessed her long-unrequited love for him. The political impediments to their union had long since evaporated and Dolly's father had been dead more than ten years. Less than two years after Elizabeth's death, Charles and Dorothy were married. Love had conquered both time and the whims of men. Or at least it seemed for the next decade.

Shortly after the birth of their seventh child, Mary, in 1724, Charles was taken aside by a trusted associate. The adviser had disturbing news, he said.

"My lord, it concerns Lady Townshend. It's your wife, sir . . ." The man's voice trailed off uncomfortably.

"Get on with it, man. What is it?" the viscount asked impatiently, his infamous temper rising.

"Sir, the lady has been seen in the company of Lord Wharton," the underling said. "It is on the lips of many in Norfolk already. A scandal is mounting."

Charles Townshend's mind reeled. Wharton? The lecherous debtor? How could she?

"Sir, Wharton's character is so infamous," the assistant continued, "no woman could be four and twenty hours under his roof with safety to her reputation. Perhaps we should—"

"Stop!" Charles shouted. He held his fist above his head as if to strike the messenger cowering before him. Instead he let his hand fall limply to his side. His shoulders slumped.

"Stop," he whispered. "Leave me."

"But my lord, what shall I tell . . ."

"Leave me," Charles repeated, and the frightened associate left. Charles knew the news could mean only one thing. His wife, who had once thrown her reputation away because she was forbidden from loving him, was doing the same thing again even though she now had the man she professed to want. His love had not been able to heal a wound she continued to salve with promiscuity and adultery.

Very well. But he was still the 2nd Viscount of Raynham, a leader in the House of Lords. He had a reputation and a family to protect. He decided right then that Dolly would never again be free to shame him or the Townshend name.

"What exactly are you saying, Charles?" Dorothy demanded of her husband.

"I'm saying you are to go to your room and remain there. You are not to leave for any purpose. I'll see to it that what you need will be brought to you there."

"What about the children? Charles, please! Don't do this!"

"The children are no longer any concern of yours. Nor is any part of this family. Go now. I won't see you again."

Just as she'd begged her father so many years ago, Dorothy cried and begged Charles for understanding, for forgiveness, for mercy, for indulgence. And just as they had before, her tears and pleas failed. Townshend family servants escorted Dorothy to her chambers, which were soon fitted with a new, soundproof door and locks that could make certain she would remain sequestered in her home confinement. She was inconsolable the rest of her days, though very few ever heard her wailing or saw her tears as she pined away for the man she loved and the children she'd borne.

Two years after the lady of Raynham Hall was locked away in her room, the word went out across Norfolk. Dorothy Townshend had died of smallpox. In the fall of 1726, a funeral was held at nearby St. Mary's Church. The services were modest considering the station of the deceased, perhaps because, as those closest to the family knew, the whole thing was a bit of theater meant to quiet incessant rumors about her affair and subsequent punishment. Dolly was not dead. She watched the procession of the empty casket from St. Mary's to the graveyard from the window of her room. Now nobody would be looking for her. She slipped deeper into her malaise and there she stayed for three more years.

In 1729, Dorothy sat on the edge of her bed as the servants unlocked her door and brought in her breakfast. While the servants were distracted, setting out her food, Dorothy in a flash bolted for the door and ran screaming down the hall. She called her children's names, hoping to catch a glimpse of them, hoping to see anyone at all. As she ran toward the main staircase, the air outside her room seemed cooler, fresher than anything she'd felt in years. The servant caught up to her at the top of the stairs and grabbed her by the arm, prepared to pull her back to her room.

Dorothy resisted.

"Please," she said, looking into the servant's eyes. Pleading. "Not back there. I can't go back in there. Please."

Whether out of mercy or out of fear of having to explain the escape, the servant released his grip on Dorothy's arm. Then, using all of his force, he pushed the slight woman down the massive staircase. The first impact on the marble steps snapped her neck, killing her. Her lifeless body tumbled down into Marble Hall just as Charles rushed in to see what the commotion was about.

Frederick Marryat was alone in the room now, staring at the Brown Lady's portrait. He found himself trying to conjure Dorothy's ghost, willing her to appear. But the room remained silent. Empty. At long last, he gave up hope of witnessing anything supernatural and began to prepare for bed. He nearly jumped out of his skin when there came a loud, insistent rapping on his chamber door.

"Who is it?" Marryat shouted.

"It is only I," his host, the young Lord Townshend, answered. "I have a request from the others in tomorrow's hunting party."

Marryat unbolted and opened the door.

"What is it?" he asked.

"A couple of the men heard about your military experience," Townshend said. "They were hoping you could bring your pistol and demonstrate how to prepare and adjust their own weapons."

Though he was only half dressed, in just trousers and vest, Marryat was anxious to get out of the room and clear his head of thoughts of women long dead. He grabbed his pistol and followed his host to a parlor where the other men were gathered. The group spent hours talking about guns and hunting.

"Well, my friends, it's well past midnight," Marryat finally said. "I'm going to retire in hopes of being fresh and rested for our morning hunt."

He walked back to his room, accompanied by Lord Townshend and two other men who continued to press the captain with last-minute questions about firearms. As they approached Marryat's room, Townshend froze. Marryat and the other men followed their host's gaze to a vision that made their blood turn to ice. A woman, glowing and translucent, was standing outside the chamber door. She turned and glared at the men, and began moving toward them.

The men cowered against the hallway wall as the woman moved silently but deliberately toward them. The ghost wore a shimmering brown dress. Marryat recognized her immediately.

"Dolly," he muttered.

At the mention of her name, the ghost turned her face directly toward the men. Her expression was a sneer of disdain and her eye sockets were empty black voids, as if her eyes had been plucked from her skull. The ghost stopped, giving the men this hard, evil glare. Marryat was so rattled, he drew his pistol and fired a single shot at the apparition. The ghost disappeared in a swirl of luminous mist. Marryat walked across the hall and dug the bullet from the woodwork, where it had lodged after it passed clean through the specter of Dorothy Townshend.

After the encounter, Captain Frederick Marryat, war hero, nautical adventurer, internationally renowned author, was so spooked he insisted on moving to a different room for the remainder of his stay at Raynham Hall. Though he'd wanted to witness the Brown Lady's ghost, the experience shook him so badly that he never wrote about the vision and rarely spoke about it except to warn others against conjuring the spirits of the dead. The face of the dead Lady Townshend haunted his nightmares until he himself passed away twelve years later in 1848.

Captain Marryat was far from the last person to see Raynham Hall's famous Brown Lady. Over the next century, sightings of Dorothy Townshend's ghost continued and her legend grew. One winter night in 1849, Major William Loftus, husband of Charles and Dorothy's daughter Elizabeth Townshend, was visiting Raynham Hall and enjoying a game of chess with a friend named Hawkins. Late into the evening, the men were finishing their match when they heard a commotion on the second floor of the estate. They mounted the stairs and turned down the hall, where they came upon a shimmering vision of a translucent woman in a brown dress.

"I know her!" Loftus managed to say before the specter vanished.

He didn't have to wait long to confirm the ghost's identity. The following evening, Major Loftus was walking the same hallway alone when he heard a faint creak behind him. Petrified, he slowly turned around to find himself face-to-face with Dolly. Frozen in horror, he could only stare at her rage-filled grimace, made all the more terrible by her empty eye sockets. It looked, he thought, as if she'd torn her own eyes out in some final rebellion against her harsh and unfair treatment. The encounter lasted close to a full minute, during which Loftus thought the angry demon might attack him. Instead, the ghost drifted slowly above him, then disappeared.

Loftus was so disturbed by this second encounter with the Raynham Hall ghost that he demanded the estate's staff work with local police to investigate. Undercover detectives were hired to live and work in the house, but, while the sightings continued, little progress was made in contacting or evicting Dorothy's ghost.

In fact, the Brown Lady continued to be so visible, she eventually caught the attention of editors at Britain's *Country Life* magazine. In September 1936, reporters were dispatched to interview witnesses and record the history that led to the haunting of Raynham Hall. But the most fateful decision was the assignment of photographer Hubert C. Provand and his assistant, Indre Shira, to try to capture the ghost on film.

On September 19, the pair set up their equipment at the foot of Raynham Hall's main stairway, the place where Dorothy is said to have died and the location of countless sightings of her ghost. They were about to make ghost-hunting history. Shira handled the mundane chores, securing tripods and lights and making sure the plates were ready for exposure. Provand took one photograph, while Shira manually flashed the lights. The photographer was focusing for another exposure while Shira stood by, flash pistol in hand, looking directly up the staircase. Suddenly an ethereal veiled form slowly descended the stairs.

"Quick!" Shira shouted. "Quick, there's something!"

Shira hit the flash, while Provand, his head still covered by the black camera drape, pushed the shutter button on faith.

"What's all the excitement about?" Provand asked when he pulled his head out from under the cloth.

Shira was speechless.

The real answer wouldn't be evident until the photographer developed the plates days later. The result of Provand and Shira's effort: the most famous ghost photo in the world. There, on Raynham Hall's main stairs, they had captured the image of a ghostly woman drifting down the staircase. The photo caused a sensation when it was published in *Country Life* magazine in December of that same year. Ever since, photography experts and ghost hunters have debated its authenticity. To some, it is clear visual evidence of the Brown Lady's existence. Critics, however, dismiss it as a double exposure, perhaps featuring a statue of the Madonna overlaid on the Raynham Hall stairway. But despite more than seventy years of investigation and high-tech examination, Provand and Shira's photo cannot be definitely proven authentic, nor can it be dismissed as a fake.

No matter what is on that photo plate, what is sure is that, in the seconds before the picture was taken, Shira saw what countless others have seen at Raynham Hall over the past three centuries.

"I yelled out because of what I saw," Shira said later. "It was the misty form of a woman. A woman who did not look happy."

Chapter 6
The Servant Girl
of St. Francis

In a different time, their love might have been one for the ages. But in the antebellum South, it was forbidden, with tragic consequences. Perhaps that's why few are allowed to rest easy in this otherwise comfortable, historic Florida bed-and-breakfast.

Even in her shapeless and drab servant's uniform, she was strikingly beautiful. Her skin glowed like burnished mahogany against the gray cotton; her eyes were sparkling onyx when she smiled. And she was nearly always smiling.

Lily's life was difficult, to be sure. Her days were filled with backbreaking chores around Teahan House. She cleaned rooms and served food, carried water and firewood, toiled in the garden, and sweated through endless loads of laundry. But Lily knew she was genuinely loved by the rest of the staff at Teahan House, a small but comfortable boardinghouse just steps from the roaring Atlantic Ocean on the Florida coast.

"Everything may be blooming here, Lily dear, but you are the real flower of this place," the head parlor maid would tell her. "Your smile is our sunshine."

Lily also knew that life for a beautiful, young girl was much better here in America than it could ever be in her native Barbados, a place she barely remembered any longer. She'd been brought to Florida when she was just a child. Her parents had told her over and over again about the one-room shack with the dirt floor that turned to mud when the incessant rains poured through the poorly thatched roof. There was never enough food. There was always the specter of disease and death. Life in America was relative paradise compared to the crushing poverty of their homeland.

The honest truth was, Lily didn't mind the hard work at Teahan House at all. She had a secret.

And so Lily smiled and worked, and doing it all under the stern, impatient gaze of Teahan House's owner, Colonel William Hardee, wasn't always easy.

Hardee, known as "Old Reliable" to his military cronies, cut an intimidating figure. He graduated from the U.S. Army Military Academy at West Point in 1838 and was a veteran of the Seminole Indian Wars and the Mexican-American War. Hardee renounced his commission when his home state of Georgia seceded from the Union in 1861. He then joined the Confederate army in charge of Fort Morgan and Fort Gaines in Alabama.

Hardee gained acclaim for leading aggressive military campaigns in the battles of Shiloh, Missionary Ridge, Perryville, and Stones River. Badly outnumbered, Hardee fought doggedly against General William T. Sherman's famed March to the Sea in Georgia, though he was eventually forced to evacuate Savannah and surrender to Sherman at Durham Station.

By 1870, Colonel Hardee was still struggling with the concept of Reconstruction. He'd settled at his family plantation near Selma, Alabama, and split his time between there and his business interests in St. Augustine, Florida. Hardee had come to own Teahan House in St. Augustine through his first wife, Elizabeth Dummett, whose family had turned the former estate into a boardinghouse in 1838.

Dummett was the daughter of former British Royal Marine Colonel Thomas Henry Dummett, a sugar and rum plantation owner who was forced to leave his native Barbados with the British outlawed slavery. He rebuilt his business in coastal Florida, smuggling many of his Barbados slaves, including Lily and her family, with him. While many of the slaves toiled in the sweltering cane fields along the Tomoka River south of the old city, a select few were chosen to work as house servants in Teahan House.

By the time Colonel Hardee came to run Teahan House, the serving staff was technically free, though their status, and their treatment under the former Confederate military officer, wasn't much different than it had been under their British slave master. Hardee never saw slavery or emancipation as the real issues behind the Civil War. Consequently, he never found the South's defeat much of a reason to change his ideas about the social order as he understood it—a social order that included vast differences in regard for those with skin of a different hue.

But he tried his best to be what he considered fair. The Teahan House staff approached him with a mix of fear and obedience.

To the rest of the world, the white world, Hardee was, outwardly at least, a successful businessman and respected war veteran. He was the author of one of the most prominent drill manuals in use at West Point as well as a history of the Irish in America. But he was a haunted man. He was still bitter about many of the things he'd seen in the war, both recklessness and incompetence on the side of the Confederates and unnecessary brutality on the side of the Union. His anger at Sherman never diminished, not just because of the general's rout of the Southern forces, but because Hardee's only son was killed fighting Sherman's army in the battle of Bentonville in North Carolina in March 1865.

Hardee sought what he'd lost in his son through his nephew, Robert Lewis, a dashing and impetuous former soldier who had taken up full-time residence in Teahan House. Hardee poured his attention on Robert and tried to counsel him in the ways of business. Robert listened patiently but often ended up cutting his uncle short.

"I appreciate your concern and your care, Colonel, I really do," Robert told his uncle one evening. "But I'm not certain I want to do business up and down the coast like you and your associates. I'm happy here. I've been thinking. What if I just stayed here and ran Teahan House for you? I'd manage it well, as if it were my own. Maybe, if I did it properly and you saw fit, it could be mine someday—"

"Nonsense," Hardee interrupted. "That's no life for a smart and adventurous man like yourself. You need to travel the world. Study abroad. Make contacts. Use your talents.

"Stay here? With the Negroes and the Old Spaniards in St. Augustine? I won't hear of it."

Robert politely excused himself. "I know you mean well, uncle. I'll think about what you've proposed. I hope you'll do the same for my wishes. For now, I'll bid you good night."

When he was out of the old man's sight, Robert looked back at his uncle, sitting alone on the porch of the old inn, looking smaller and frailer as the years wore away at the facade of military officer and war hero. It would break his uncle's heart to hear the real reason he wanted to stay here in St. Augustine, Robert thought. If he knew why a strapping young man with powerful connections would be satisfied as a simple innkeeper, he'd be furious.

He would cross that bridge when he came to it, Robert decided. Right now, he had a commitment to keep.

Robert climbed to the inn's second floor, comforted by the easy creak of the old place with each step. When he got to the end of the hall, he found the door to the Teahan's Ballerina Room slightly ajar. He smiled. He pushed the door open and saw that a fire was blazing in the room's tiny, paneled fireplace. Crazy shadows played on the wall and he felt the heat wash over him as he stepped into the orange light filling the room.

"Are you here?" he called.

No answer.

He made a show of looking around the room, peering under the bed and behind the drapes. Finally he heard a giggle from the shadows behind the massive wardrobe.

"It's time for my flower to come into the light," Robert whispered.

She stepped from the shadows and into the warm glow of the fire. Smooth brown skin, ebony hair, and sparkling eyes. She smiled and it melted him.

"Lily," he managed weakly.

"I love you, Robert," she said quietly.

She came to him and he held her. By the fire in an empty lodging room, they professed their love again and again. It was for this that Lily managed every task with a smile here at Teahan. It was for this that Robert was willing to forsake his uncle's aid and success in international business and settle for a simple life in St. Augustine.

As they had many times before, they let their passions overwhelm them and spent long hours in their lover's embrace.

✦

Downstairs, still unnerved by the conversation with his nephew, Colonel Hardee decided he needed to know once and for all what was holding Robert back. *I love him as if he were my own son,* he thought. *I could not want more for my own, dear departed boy than I want for Robert. He must be made to see that leaving this place is what's best for him.*

It was late now, well past midnight. Hardee decided it couldn't wait. He'd visit the boy in his room and talk to him, reason with him. The colonel started slowly climbing to Robert's attic bedroom on the third floor of the inn. He stopped to rest on the second-floor landing. He heard faint voices coming from down the hall. *There are no guests in that part of the building,* he thought. Probably some of the servants engaged in some illicit behavior. He decided to delay his conversation with Robert long enough to put a stop to whatever was going on.

As he approached the Ballerina Room, Hardee clearly heard the voices of a man and a woman. His rage was building. What in God's name were the servants thinking, behaving like this? Without knocking, Colonel Hardee burst into the room to give the miscreants what for.

When his eyes adjusted to the dim firelight, he was dumbstruck. There before him were the stunned, horrified figures of his nephew and Lily, the normally effervescent servant girl.

"Uncle!" Robert cried.

Colonel Hardee turned and walked silently out of the room. He paused in the doorway, then, out of modesty, closed the door behind him.

The following day, Teahan House throbbed with the sound of sobbing as Lily was led away by several of Colonel Hardee's employees. She was no longer a house servant, the staff was told. She was being taken to the cane plantation, where she would remain in his employ as a field servant, assuming she could survive the horrid work in the tropical heat. Lily's fellow servants were despondent over the loss of the girl who was the bright spot in most of their lives. They begged Colonel Hardee to reconsider, but he flatly refused.

Robert made an impassioned appeal to his uncle as well.

"You've said you love me as your flesh and blood," Robert wailed. "You must see that you are tearing out my heart bit by bit. Uncle, please, don't do this thing. This woman, Lily, she is everything to me. Haven't I always been good and loyal to you and your interests?"

"You cavort with slaves and refuse my requests to better yourself," his uncle replied coldly. "I fail to see how any of this is in my interest, unless my interest is in the humiliation of my family and the dismissal of everything I've ever fought for."

Robert was stunned, furious.

"You tired, pathetic old man. You can't possibly understand, can you?"

"I understand this much. Of all the things I've ever done for you, my nephew, I saved the most important and valuable one for today. You'll weep for this black wench for a week or two, but you'll be thanking me for a lifetime for rescuing you from your disastrous urges."

"I have no thanks, now or ever," Robert seethed. "I have nothing but curses for you in this life and the next."

Colonel Hardee sequestered himself in his room for the next few days, chewing on his anger over his nephew's actions and the ungrateful lad's rebuke. The old man was taking his dinner in his chamber on the third night after the blowup when a servant burst in, breathless with fear and excitement.

"Colonel, come quick!" the maid shouted. "It's Master Robert. Oh, please, sir, come quick!"

Hardee bolted from his chair and followed the screaming woman up to Robert's third-floor room. The door was open. Hardee had to push aside several wailing chambermaids to see into the room. And then he saw. There swung the lifeless body of his nephew. He'd hanged himself with a length of carriage rope tied to an exposed rafter in the attic bedroom. He'd been dead for hours. Dark purple blotches obscured his handsome face. As if the young man had doubts in the final seconds of the horrid act, both hands were tucked tightly between the rope and his distended neck, the fingertips already turning black from the fatal pressure.

"What have I done?" the colonel grunted. He ran to the young man's corpse and pulled it down from the noose. As he'd done with his own son years before, he held the cold body close to his and wept bitter tears.

In the years that followed the tragedy of lost love at Teahan House, the place took on a morose tone. Hardee himself went back to Selma, never to return. He fell ill during a summer vacation in West Virginia in 1873 and died shortly thereafter. Hardee's sister-in-law, Anna Dummett, continued to run the place until 1888, when she sold it to prominent Florida philanthropist and developer John L. Wilson. The place took on several names as various owners tried to make a go of it in historic St. Augustine. Over the years Teahan House came to be known as Hudson House, Valencia Annex, Amity House, Salt Air Apartments, The Palms, Graham House, and finally the St. Francis Inn.

As for Lily, it is said she perished shortly after she was banished, in part from the harsh conditions and in part due to a broken heart. She was never told about Robert's death by his own hand, which likely explains why, some 140 years hence, she continues to search for her man, the object of her forbidden love.

These days, the St. Francis Inn is a favorite spot for couples, older folks on second honeymoons, and young lovers on romantic getaways, all enjoying the laid-back, beachy vibe of St. Augustine. So Victor felt a little out of place checking in by himself.

"I'm a writer. I'm working on a book. A book about famous people and their pets," he told the young clerk without being asked. "This seemed, I don't know, like a nice, quiet spot to get some work done."

"It certainly is, sir," the cheerful girl replied. "We'll make certain you are not disturbed, if that's what you'd like. And I've put you in our most comfortable room on the top floor, where it's always quiet. You're in Lily's Room, number 3-A. Here's your key. Will there be anything else at the moment?"

"No. No, thank you," Victor replied. He felt foolish for volunteering his purpose to the clerk. He probably seemed odd enough walking in here alone, he thought. Now he was making it worse with his awkward explanations.

"I'm fine," he added.

It didn't occur to him to ask why his room had a name, and a woman's name at that. He assumed it was some quirk of the St. Francis. He grabbed his bags and made his way up to the inn's attic room, anxious to unpack, take in the harbor view from the third floor, and perhaps get some work done before dinner.

He unlocked the whitewashed, paneled door and walked into a cozy, slightly over-furnished room dominated by a massive Tudor four-poster bed of hand-tooled ash. The Bahama shutters on the floor-to-ceiling windows let in shards of dappled sunlight that made the emerald carpet in Lily's Room glow like the surface of a tropical lagoon. Victor smiled. It was everything he'd hoped for on this trip.

As he unpacked, he kept getting a sense of movement in the far corners of his vision. Just reflections in the glossy punched-tin ceiling, he told himself. He ignored the sensation and placed his things around the room. When he was fully unpacked, he took off his shoes and stretched out on the bed, feeling the cooling rush from the ceiling fan. That's when he saw her for the first time. It started as nothing more than a shadow, like some disturbance in the light from an object passing by outside his window. But as the shadow moved slowly across the room, it became more solid, more defined. It was here in the room with him. It was a young girl. A beautiful young black girl in a simple servant's dress. She floated soundlessly across the room right before Victor's eyes and dissolved just as she'd appeared.

Victor couldn't move. With the vision gone, he immediately began to doubt he'd seen anything at all. He was tired, after all, he told himself. He'd been traveling for days to get to St. Augustine. He considered rushing downstairs to tell someone at the front desk. *No,* he thought, *they already think I'm an oddball, coming here by myself with my stories about books and writing. I'm just tired and slipped into a dream while napping. That's all.*

He spent the rest of the evening alone in his room, trying to work, but mostly distracted by the memory of the shadowy figure he'd seen and the continuing sense that things were moving in the room just out of his sight. Around midnight, he retired, pulling the heavy down comforter up to his chin as a damp, chilly breeze blew in off the ocean and filled Lily's Room.

At some time during the night, Victor dreamed that he was being buried alive. That he was wrapped in a death shroud and placed in a coffin of polished ash. He tried his best to protest, but the funeral party couldn't hear him. They nailed him shut inside his casket, where he gasped for air and tried in vain to move. The horrible dream woke him up, but when Victor opened his eyes, the reality was as bad as the nightmare. He was still trapped. Though his eyes were open, the world was still pitch black. He was wrapped like a mummy, bound in the down comforter, his head resting on hard wood. As his heart raced, he felt the heat of his own breath being reflected back into his face. Just above his nose and continuing well beyond the length and width of his body, more polished wood hemmed him in. He seemed, indeed, to be trapped in a coffin.

It was several hours before two St. Francis chambermaids making their early rounds heard the weak, muffled cries coming from Lily's Room. After knocking and failing to get anything more than moans and grunts in reply, the maids summoned a manager who entered 3-A with a pass key.

"Sir, are you okay?" the manager shouted into the darkened room.

"Please help me," Victor said weakly.

It took the manager and the maids almost a full minute to find their guest. When they did, they were dumbstruck.

Victor was bound in the hotel comforter and wedged tightly, face up, under the enormous four-poster bed. As the perimeter of the bed frame was less than six inches from the floor, there was not enough room to slide Victor out from underneath. The St. Francis employees tried to lift the bed, but it was too heavy for the three adults to lift. Victor was beginning to panic. He thrashed around feebly under the bed as his claustrophobia mounted. He begged to be freed.

Finally, the St. Francis manager called the local fire department. It took a team of a half dozen strapping St. Augustine firefighters to pull Victor out from under the bed in Lily's Room. He left the inn that afternoon, never to return. His book, as far as anyone knows, was never published.

Victor's story is just part of the ghostly lore at the St. Francis Inn, almost all of which involves Lily and her lost love. Inn employees and guests have for decades reported sightings of both the beautiful servant girl and her dashing young soldier. The girl is usually silent and dressed all in light gray. And while the story of the guest trapped under the bed may be the most popular St. Francis ghost story, Lily's favorite target actually seems to be other young women in love.

One woman staying in Lily's Room told the staff she and her husband were awakened in the middle of the night by a loud thud. She rose to investigate and found the contents of her pocketbook scattered across the floor. Nothing was missing, but her cosmetic bag was completely filled with water.

And it's not just Lily who haunts the old inn. A number of guests have reported seeing the figure of a lone, forlorn soldier peering down from the third-floor windows. Many guess it is Robert, who continues to search in vain for Lily just as she continues to seek him. That would help explain the experience of one young woman who was staying in the St. Francis on her honeymoon several years ago. The new bride was awakened by a passionate kiss. Eyes still closed, she reached out to embrace her husband but found no one there. She opened her eyes to find him fast asleep beside her.

When she reported the incident to the staff later that day, they told her the story of Lily and Robert and Colonel Hardee. Rather than being frightened, the young woman was intrigued by the amount of love that seemed to still be flowing in the old boardinghouse. It was a fitting place, she thought, for a honeymoon.

"I think that love that begins here lasts forever," the new bride said. "I only wish they could find one another and feel once again what I've felt here."

Chapter 7
Anna of Savannah

Heartbroken and cheated, a naive young girl is driven beyond her limits as she watches her lothario sail away from her forever. To this day, she inhabits the Savannah, Georgia, house where she once waited for the return of her one true love.

Anna looked out the third-floor window of the old inn and cried silent tears. From here she could see the ships leaving the Savannah port and following the river out to the open sea. Her tears rolled off her chin and landed on her belly, which was just beginning to show the swell of the child she was carrying inside. His child. She opened the window and climbed out onto the narrow ledge, wanting to see the masts of his ship, wanting to see the amber sails under which they'd first fallen in love.

Six months earlier, in the spring of 1831, the world seemed a much brighter place to Anna Powers. She and her sister, Elizabeth, were finally starting to get over the grief that came when their beloved father had died the previous autumn. Their father had raised them by himself since their mother had died when they were very young. Losing him not only hurt, it severed their one and only tie to rural England, the only place on earth they had ever known.

With their mourning behind them, they packed up their few belongings and left the English countryside, headed for the British coast. There they spent what little money they'd inherited to book passage on a Portuguese schooner bound for America. As Anna climbed aboard the crowded ship, she felt a rush of hope for her future like she'd never experienced. She also caught one of the handsome young mates balanced precariously in the ship's rigging smiling down at her. She stole a glance. His blond hair had gone almost completely white from the sun. His bare arms were as solid and powerful as the massive wooden mast he clung to. And yet, when he shifted his weight and moved along the yardarm to keep his view of Anna as she walked through the mass of passengers, his movements were easy, graceful, controlled.

He smiled. Anna was hypnotized. She didn't notice that her sister had stopped moving to let a mother with two small children pass in front of her. Anna pushed her suitcase into the back of Elizabeth's legs.

"Watch where you're going!" Elizabeth shouted.

"Sorry. I'm sorry." Anna giggled. She looked up to see the seaman laughing and turning away. Her heart sank a little.

Elizabeth followed her sister's gaze up into the rigging.

"Anna! Stop it right now! I mean it. We're going to be stuck on this boat for five weeks, and that's if we're lucky. You need to concentrate on staying healthy and getting through this trip. Nothing good can come from making eyes at the ship's help. For goodness' sake, we haven't even left the dock yet!"

"Oh, please," Anna protested. "Don't you think I know all that? I was just looking at the sails, that's all. But Beth, honestly, wasn't he cute?"

Both girls broke up laughing. Their joking was interrupted by angry shouts behind them. Impatient passengers ordered them to move along now that the path to the lower decks was clear. Anna scanned the boat one more time, looking for the white-haired mate. He was gone. *No matter,* she thought. *It's going to be a long trip on a fairly small ship.* She would see him again. With renewed enthusiasm, she made her way to the narrow bunk that would serve as her living quarters for the remainder of the arduous journey to America.

If the United States was the land of opportunity, simply getting there was the dues required for a chance at the American dream, Anna knew. She'd read much about crossing the Atlantic before she agreed to make this trip, and she was well aware of the hardships she and Elizabeth would face. Even with the prevailing westerly winds, the passage could last as long as two months. In that time, the sisters would be treated to crowded, noisy, foul-smelling confinement ridden with all manner of vermin. Food and water, amenities they'd paid handsomely for, would be stale at best and contaminated at worst. With no medical care and no thought given to hygiene or sanitation, the chance of illness and even death were great.

Anna looked around at the mass of passengers—old people, poor families with dirty-faced children—and was amazed at the faith shown by all of these folks. They were about to embark on the most difficult adventure of their lives in hopes of finding new fortunes in a place they'd only read about.

On their sixth day at sea, Anna's queasiness, brought on by the rolling waves, had subsided. She managed to eat a few hard, salty biscuits, washing them down with the cloudy water being passed from bunk to bunk in an oak bucket. She looked down at poor Elizabeth, who was still suffering intense nausea that confined her to her bunk. Anna decided to venture onto the main deck to feel the fresh, salt air on her skin for the first time since she'd left England.

"I'll be right back," Anna said as she wiped the clammy sweat from her sister's forehead and straightened the miserable girl's matted hair.

Anna climbed the rickety ladder and emerged from the hatch into a world that was startlingly, painfully bright. Sunlight sparkled on the wave tops as far as she could see through squinted eyes. The wind whipped the lines in the rigging into a humming chorus. Anna steadied herself against the rail and took it all in. Her hair blew wild behind her, mimicking the mast pennants high above her head. She felt the schooner list farther to port as they sliced through a sea so big it stole her breath.

Swept up in her ocean reverie, she never saw the young mate approaching her from behind.

"She's quite beautiful, isn't she?" he said.

Anna jumped at the sound of his voice. Startled and a little annoyed to be shaken from her daydream, she turned to face the interloper and found herself staring into eyes as strikingly blue as the sea surrounding her. It was the seaman she'd seen on the day she boarded. Up close he seemed bigger, younger, more of everything she'd sensed when she first watched him move easily across the yard and spar. He brushed a mass of that blond-white hair out of his face with a callused hand and smiled at her.

"I frightened you. I'm sorry," he said in a thick Austrian accent. "My name is Hans. I am the boatswain. I saw you when you came aboard, but I lost sight of you and haven't seen you since."

"I've been a little seasick, but I'm better now," she offered, reaching out to shake his hand. "I am Anna. I'm going to America with my sister. What's a boatswain?"

"I take care of equipment and maintenance on the ship," he answered. "If you are ever in need of something, perhaps I can help—"

"Is this your method with all the young women onboard?"

Anna interrupted, smiling. She was teasing him. "To charm them and see who might trade their affections for an extra ration of hard tack?"

Hans blushed but kept his eyes fixed on Anna's. "Never, Miss. A gentleman of the sea wouldn't stoop so low. And besides, the captain controls all of the dry goods."

They both laughed.

"Tell me about where we're going," Anna said.

Until late in the afternoon, Hans thrilled Anna with stories about Savannah and the Georgia coast. It was a place, the young Austrian said, of both immense riches and stark poverty, of hope and intrigue and danger. Pious Presbyterian ministers walked the city streets side-by-side with grizzled fishermen and bloodthirsty pirates. Hans told her how the place was still recovering from two yellow fever outbreaks that had killed thousands, and a fire in 1820 that nearly burned the entire city flat. But despite its trouble, Hans, who by then had seen much of the American coast, said there was nothing like Savannah's mix of genteel Southern culture, Caribbean-flavored voodoo, and salty, nautical sensibilities.

"I think you and your sister shall do quite well there," Hans said.

The ship was now pointed directly into the setting sun, and to Anna, it seemed like the world had been set ablaze. Even the ocean burned deep red and orange. "I should get back to my sister now. She'll be convinced I fell overboard," Anna said. She took Hans's hand lightly in hers. "Thank you for your stories, and your kindness. I should like to speak with you again."

"I'm never far away," Hans said, smiling.

"Where have you been? You've been gone for hours!" Elizabeth shouted.

"It's a beautiful day, Beth. You should see it," Anna responded. "Are you feeling any better?"

"A bit. Did you get any word on our progress? How close are we to America?"

"You know what? I never asked. I have no idea."

Anna began to regale her sister with all that she'd learned about Savannah and what a wonderful life they were going to have there once they arrived. Elizabeth scowled as Anna's description of the Georgia coast became more vivid and detailed.

"Who told you all this?" she finally demanded.

"I spoke to a gentleman with much experience in the city of Savannah. He was quite helpful and encouraging."

Elizabeth stared into Anna's eyes. "You went up there to find your blond sailor boy, didn't you?"

"Oh, Beth, he's so warm and kind, and his eyes . . . I could have listened to him talk about his adventures forever. I left him five minutes ago and I'm already dying to see him again.."

Elizabeth rolled over in her bunk with a grunt. "I believe I'm feeling sick again," she mumbled.

Despite her sister's protestations, Anna continued to meet with Hans every afternoon. What began simply as the two huddling in some quiet part of the ship, sharing their heart's desires, blossomed somewhere midway across the Atlantic Ocean into a full-blown love affair. Three weeks into the voyage, it was not unusual to see Hans and Anna walking the deck hand-in-hand, or slipping below to the equipment storerooms Hans controlled for more private romantic encounters. Anna took the whispers and snickering of Hans's fellow crewmates as nothing more than petty jealousy. Anna told Elizabeth that Hans had promised to marry her when they got to Savannah.

"None of this strikes you as unusual at all?" Elizabeth asked. "You've taken up with a man you hardly know in the middle of this miserable boat ride and now you're talking about marriage? What would our father make of all this?"

"Oh hush, Beth. He loves me. Is that so hard to fathom? I'm going to be the wife of a handsome sailor in America and we're going to have beautiful blond children who will grow up strong and adventurous like their father."

"So now it's children you're talking about, Anna. A bit soon for that, isn't it? Have you lost all of your sense?"

Anna sat on the edge of Elizabeth's bunk and took her sister's hand, placing it against her stomach. She kept her voice low so the others in the tight quarters wouldn't hear.

"It's not too soon at all," Anna whispered. "I think it's already done. I'm sure our child is already inside me."

On the forty-first day after they left England, Anna and Elizabeth heard shouting from the deck above them, followed by a stampede of footsteps rushing toward the bow of the ship. The sisters scrambled above to see what the commotion was about.

"Are we sinking?" Elizabeth asked an agitated group of passengers trying to push their way forward.

"No, foolish girl. We're arriving! The word has gone out that land is in sight! Praise the good Lord, we're coming to our new home!"

Anna and Elizabeth shouted with happiness and hugged each other. All around them, passengers cried and prayed and lifted children over their heads so the young ones could get their first glimpse of America.

Anna saw Hans and ran to him, trying to embrace him, but he pushed her aside.

"Now is not the time," he told her, strangely detached. "Approaching the coast requires the attention of the entire crew. I'm sorry. I must work now. We'll meet on the docks after the ship is secured."

"I understand," said Anna. She pouted a little. But it made sense, she thought to herself. The crew had to bring the schooner in safely. To the crew, the ship came first. If she was going to be a sailor's wife, she needed to understand these things.

When they arrived at the Savannah pier, Elizabeth went on ahead to a rooming house recommended to them by a fellow passenger. Anna waited for Hans, but even several hours later the crew was still busy coiling lines, stowing sails, and securing countless pieces of the ship's gear. When she finally caught a glimpse of her lover, she shouted from the edge of the dock.

"Hans, dearest. I'm going to find my sister. Will you find me when your work is done?"

A few of the deckhands snickered. She ignored them. Hans came close to the gunwale to speak with her.

"Where are you staying?" he asked her.

"At the Steele White house on Presidents Street. Do you know it?"

"I do. I know it well. Go there and I'll meet you tomorrow. We'll be at our work here for the rest of the night."

Saddened, Anna turned away and walked the four blocks from the dock to the boardinghouse with her head down. She knew she should be ecstatic about arriving in America. She should be marveling in the incredible sights, sounds, and smells of bustling Savannah. If nothing else, she should be rejoicing to be on dry land after six weeks of being tossed about on the Atlantic. But all she could think about was Hans. How she wanted to be with him. To hold him. To keep him near to her. She hadn't yet told him about the baby growing inside her. In the past few weeks of the journey, she'd passed off her incessant nausea as a recurrence of her seasickness.

Only Anna and Elizabeth knew the truth.

At the Steele White house, Anna found Elizabeth already settling in to a room on the third floor. It was a small but comfortable place with a fireplace and huge windows that faced the Savannah River. Anna dropped her things on the floor and went to the windows. In the waning light, she thought she could just make out the mainmast of the ship that had brought her and Elizabeth and the man she would soon marry safely to shore. She began to relax. In short order, both sisters were enjoying the deepest sleep they'd known in nearly two months.

The next morning, Elizabeth was anxious to explore their new city. Anna, however, was content to wait in their room for Hans, who had promised to meet her there. Reluctantly, Elizabeth left her sister behind.

"I'm sure he'll be here soon," she said with little conviction.

"He'll be here," Anna said confidently.

As Elizabeth made her way through the narrow lanes surrounding the boardinghouse, she came across a tavern where a raucous group was spending the morning getting blind drunk. The doors were open and the hooligans spilled out onto the sidewalk, where they made great sport of hooting and beckoning to Elizabeth as she walked past. The young girl did her best to ignore them. As she neared the corner, she stole a look back at the waterfront toughs and was stunned by what she saw. A young sailor, his bright blond hair falling about his broad shoulders, stood among the crowd. In one hand he held a pewter mug of ale. His other arm was firmly about the waist of a buxom young brunette who was busy leading the group in drunken song.

Furious, Elizabeth marched up to Hans and confronted him.

"What is the meaning of this?" she asked, pointing to the woman on his arm.

Hans stared mutely. The brunette answered for him.

"I'll tell you what the meaning is," the young woman spat. "I'm his wife and I'm celebrating my husband's return from a long voyage. Why? Did he promise to marry you if you kept him company at sea?"

The entire tavern erupted in laughter. Elizabeth, fuming, waited for the din to die down.

"I wouldn't have accepted his company if my very life depended on it," she replied. She turned to Hans. "My sister, however, grew quite close to you in anticipation of you keeping your word to marry her. She's not only waiting for you at this moment, but she's also pregnant with your child. Have you no shame, sir?"

Hans's wife reached out to slap Elizabeth's face, but, to the crowd's great disappointment, Hans intervened.

"Tell your sister I'm sorry," he said. "Love means something different at sea than it does on dry land. I thought she understood."

Humiliated, Elizabeth turned away and returned to the Steele White house. She found Anna there sitting among her few meager possessions, waiting patiently for the man she loved to come and find her. Elizabeth was heartbroken. She began to weep.

"Beth, what's wrong?"

"Oh, Anna, I'm so sorry."

With that, Beth recounted the entire encounter with Hans and his bride. How the callous seaman's wife had dismissed his indiscretions and mocked the woman he'd hurt. She told her sister how Hans had casually regarded their romance as a convenient affair of the sea and that he felt nothing for her now. Worst of all, Elizabeth told her how his face had remained blank, expressionless when he heard that she was pregnant.

Anna was too stunned to cry.

For the next few weeks, Anna barely left her room at the Steele White. Devastated, she couldn't bear the thought of seeing Hans somewhere on the streets, perhaps in the company of his wife. She lay in the dark, a stranger's child growing inside her, wondering why God had brought her so far for so much misery. Fifteen days after they landed, Elizabeth came back to the room with news. Hans's ship would be leaving port the next morning for a return trip to Europe. Maybe Anna could at last get out and see the city without fear of running into him. But Anna seemed uninterested. When the next morning arrived, Anna asked Elizabeth to get her some pastries and fresh fruit for breakfast. It was an errand, Anna knew, that would take some time to accomplish.

Elizabeth was happy to comply, thinking perhaps her spirits were rising along with her appetite.

It was only after her sister left the room that Anna made her way to the window.

And now, here she was, crying silently to herself as she balanced on the ledge outside her window three stories above the brick garden walkway that encircled the Steele White house. At last, through the trees and between the rooftops that stood between her and the docks, she spotted the amber sails of Hans's ship. She watched the schooner back slowly from its berth, then make its way along with the current down the Savannah River. Tender moments she'd spent with Hans during their voyage flooded her thoughts. The tips of the sails turned eastward at the mouth of the river and made for the open sea. Anna kept her eye on them until the last glimpse of the ship disappeared below the horizon.

From somewhere deep within her, a scream started. It built until she could no longer contain it and it came rushing out of her with full force. Her scream echoed off the stone and clapboard buildings around her and came back to her ears doubled. She screamed until she was breathless. When she was done screaming, she jumped. She landed on the bricks below, crushing her head and snapping her neck and stopping the beating of her already broken heart. Anna Powers was dead. But she was not gone.

Robert Dana is a hydrologist, a man of science. It would be charitable to say he was dismissive of the ghost stories he heard from colleagues who had visited Savannah as part of their work at the nearby Savannah River Plant near Aiken, South Carolina. Nearly all of what he heard revolved around the old Steele White boardinghouse in Savannah, a place that had long ago been renamed the 17 Hundred 90 Inn. Robert got an earful of the life and lost love of Anna Powers. He didn't believe a word of it. So when, during check-in about twelve years ago, a clerk looked at him nervously and asked if he minded taking room 204 at the 17 Hundred 90, he couldn't stifle a chuckle.

"Why would I mind?" he asked. "Isn't one room much like the next?"

"Well, outwardly they are, sir. Certainly," the desk clerk replied. "But 204 is known here as Anna's Room. It's where she ended her life. And where she continues her haunting."

"I'll be fine," Robert said. "Just give me the key. I'm tired and I'd like to relax, if that's okay with you . . . and Anna."

The clerk laughed uncomfortably and finished checking Robert in.

Late that evening, Robert was roused from a deep sleep by the unmistakably gentle caress of a woman's hand along the length of his body. He felt the seductive fingertips tracing a slow line from his forehead to his ankles. And then, a kiss. Warm lips on his. Soft at first, then deeper, more passionate. Robert sighed and surrendered to the erotic intrusion. In his dream state, he had no idea where he was. He thought for a moment that his wife was waking him in an amorous mood, and he reached to embrace her in reciprocation.

His hands found nothing but the empty bed beside him. Fully awake and startled now, Robert tried to make sense of what had just happened. Something caught his eye. Through the sheer drapes on the large windows, he could see a shape silhouetted in the moonlight. It was the figure of a woman standing on the ledge outside his widow. Robert was frozen in fear. He watched as the shape floated back and forth, its shadow, projected on the curtains, distorted only slightly by the feeble evening breeze.

There had to be some logical explanation for this, Robert thought. He sprang from the bed, meaning to rush and throw open the drapes to expose the source of the creepy vision. But as soon as he reached the window, a piercing scream filled the room. Robert paused and watched in horror as the shadow fell from sight, as if plunging to the courtyard below. He opened the blinds and looked at the ground beneath his window. Nothing.

Though it was well after midnight, he did what dozens of guests assigned to the 17 Hundred 90 Inn's room 204 do. Robert Dana, man of science, packed all of his things and went downstairs to the night clerk asking to be moved to another room.

Employees at the 17 Hundred 90 say such encounters with Anna's ghost are so common, they hardly raise eyebrows any longer. Tales abound of inn staff members and guests hearing the moaning and wailing of Anna as she re-creates her fatal fall. Many have seen Anna, a beautiful, fine-featured girl with long dark hair, reflected in the inn's mirrors and windows. Others have witnessed her spirit floating in the stairwell and hallway adjacent to room 204.

Most striking, Anna continues to treat the men and women who visit the 17 Hundred 90 very differently. The men, as Robert Dana can attest, are generally approached with great affection. Several years before Robert's encounter, a husband and wife staying in room 204 came back to their room after a long, hot day of touring greater Savannah's numerous tourist sites. Tempers flared when the couple couldn't agree on where to have dinner, and the argument carried over into the evening. When it came time to retire, the wife told her husband he wasn't welcome in the room's comfortable, four-poster bed. He could help himself to the small couch in the corner, however.

And so he did. He tossed and turned for several hours trying to get comfortable before finally falling into a fitful sleep in the wee hours of the morning. Sometime before dawn, he was roused by the feeling of soft, loving kisses on his neck and face. Thrilled that his wife was eager to put their row behind them, he pulled her close in the dark and they kissed and cuddled through the remaining darkness. When he awoke the next morning, he found himself alone on the couch and assumed his wife had returned to the comfort of the bed at some point in the night.

When she awoke, he thanked her for her kindness and her passion and for being so eager to put the fight behind them. She scowled at him, clearly still angry from the previous night, and asked him what he was talking about.

He told her, in detail, what he'd experienced the night before.

"I was certain it was you," he swore.

It most certainly was not her, she shot back. And having a romantic encounter with a ghost did nothing to help heal the rift between them, she added.

If men are treated to loving touches and passionate kisses, women are met more often with aggressive disdain when they cross paths with Anna Powers's ghost. Women sleeping in room 204 at the 17 Hundred 90 say they've been pushed right out of bed onto the floor. Others have found their clothing missing and their makeup trashed. And the one thing Anna loves to steal most of all? Guests' underwear, which frequently turns up in embarrassing locations around the inn, such as planters in the lobby or on the shelves behind the front desk.

Lights in the inn flicker on and off whenever guests invoke Anna's name. Televisions emit sound even when turned off, and guests receive ghostly telephone calls with only a sobbing woman on the other end of the line. In the dining area at the 17 Hundred 90, glasses explode in the presence of beautiful women. And loving young couples, who often seek out the 17 Hundred 90 for honeymoons or romantic getaways, are favorite targets of lovelorn Anna's spirit.

One young bride was awakened by the feeling of water dripping on her face. She opened her eyes to find the ghostly image of Anna Powers hovering over the bed. Anna's eyes were swollen and red from crying and her tears were rolling off her spectral face, soaking the young newlywed. She sprung from the bed just as the sad, horrific specter disappeared. When she shook her young husband awake, he was surprised as she threw her arms around him and clung to his neck. He felt the damp tears on her face, which he assumed were hers.

"What's the matter?" he asked. "Have you been crying?"

"It wasn't me, it was her," his bride answered cryptically. "I think it's proof."

"Proof? Proof of what?" he asked.

"Of our love," she said, smiling. "The ghost would know for sure. She knows how much we love each other."

Chapter 8
The Ghost
at the Throttle

The engineer knew it was a forbidden love, and yet he was driven to pursue her. In the end, a jealous ghost and a hurtling train on the outskirts of London settled the score with horrific certainty.

James Brierly was a haunted man. By the early 1930s, he'd become one of the most experienced and reliable engineers working for the old London, Midland and Scottish Railway. Lately, however, he was barely able to stand erect at the end of his midnight runs. White as a sheet, he'd stagger from the engine and hold his tired head in his hands, unable to fully explain what was troubling him.

Rumors began about Brierly's sanity. It was not the first time the engineer had been the subject of accusatory whispers. This time, Brierly thought, he needed to tell someone, to tell anyone, about what was happening to him on that cursed train every night. Perhaps that could help bring an end to the horrible thing he'd started when he first began to fall in love with another man's wife.

Brierly sought out William John Warner, an Irishman who, at the time, went by the alias Cheiro. Warner, or Cheiro, claimed to be an astrologer, a clairvoyant, a palmist, and an expert on all things paranormal. Cheiro had become world famous reading palms and predicting the future for dignitaries and celebrities like Mark Twain, Oscar Wilde, Grover Cleveland, and Thomas Edison, among others. Gaining an audience with Cheiro normally would have been beyond the means of a simple man like James Brierly. But as Cheiro was collecting stories for a book of spiritual encounters called *True Ghost Stories*—and because the engineer made such a heartfelt plea to the famous occult expert—the two men met to discuss Brierly's ghost problems.

"First, do you believe the dead can return?" Brierly asked Cheiro.

Cheiro pondered the question for a moment, wondering what, if any, help he'd be able to offer this man.

"I do believe the so-called dead can return and do return under certain conditions," the mystic finally answered. "I've had many personal experiences that prove it."

"Then I am not mad!" Brierly shouted. "Thank God I have found someone to whom I can speak of this."

With that, Brierly launched into a detailed account of his career on the trains in and around London and of the special relationship he had with his mentor, a fellow engineer named Robson, who was, by Brierly's own reckoning, one of the finest men employed by the LMS rail line. Robson was responsible for Brierly's success. Robson trained Brierly and gave him advice, and the older man used his influence in the company to make certain Brierly was always at the top of the list to be considered for promotions. Brierly worked his way up from serving as Robson's fireman on the Midnight Express to becoming a driver in his own right, running trains on the local circuit.

Brierly returned Robson's support with faithful friendship and loyalty. When Robson made plans to wed his fiancée, Margaret, he wanted Brierly as the best man. The two became inseparable in and out of work. Shortly after he and Margaret were married, Robson bought a cottage along one of the local rail lines outside London. The little house was right beside the first stop on Brierly's local train route.

Robson frequently brought his young wife into the rail yard. One night, after visiting with Brierly and the crew, Robson was due back aboard the Midnight Express. He asked Brierly to see his wife home to the cottage along the local line.

"I was as proud as any man could be," Brierly told Cheiro. "I saw Robson's wife to her door. I told her how much I owed to Robson. And we both agreed that Robson was the best chap on earth."

That should have been the end of it. But as Brierly now knew, it was the beginning of the end. The chivalrous errand was followed by several casual visits. Over time, Brierly found himself stopping by the railside cottage every day. It was just talk, Brierly insisted. Yet, he couldn't deny a growing obsession with his dearest friend's wife.

Within a year, Robson and Margaret had a beautiful baby girl. But still, Brierly's regular rendezvous continued. Brierly began making extended stops of an hour or more at the station near Robson's house, and the innocent visits to share a few friendly words became a great deal more. The other railway workers began to talk and their gossip reached Robson's ears, but Brierly seemed powerless to stop.

"I would not allow myself to think that I was in love with Robson's wife," he said. "I believed I would have killed myself before I did anything dishonorable. But the yearning and the longing for her grew until, in the end, it twisted every thought of honor or manhood I possessed."

Robson finally confronted Brierly. He knew what was going on, he said. Robson insisted Brierly request a transfer from the local line to another train. If he didn't, if he persisted in his clandestine meetings with Margaret, Robson swore, Brierly would suffer the consequences.

"I will have my revenge," Robson said ominously before turning on his heels and walking away, leaving Brierly alone and shaken in the rail yard.

Brierly complied. He sought a transfer from the LMS supervisors and was put on the Midlands. His new train traveled on the same main line past Margaret's cottage, but without stopping. The change drove him closer to insanity. Despite having a wife and daughter of his own at home, Brierly pined for Margaret, slowing his train to a crawl when he hit the sweeping bend that passed her house, hoping to catch a glimpse of her by day, or to see a lantern signaling him by night.

Margaret reciprocated. She waved and signaled whenever she could. The physical separation only made the two of them more reckless in their illicit affair. Brierly began to write to Margaret, long, passionate notes expressing his desire for her. He didn't care any longer whether Robson found the letters or knew about their relationship.

"It was no use trying to pull myself together," James Brierly told his spiritual confessor. "I had gone too far. Separation had intensified my torment until life became a living hell."

That living hell was about to get much worse.

One Saturday evening, Brierly approached the bend near the cottage, where he expected to see a lantern bidding him goodnight. But the porch was pitch dark. He laid on the train's whistle as he'd done many nights previous, hoping to get some response from Margaret. Still, the little cottage remained dark. Brierly got a sickly sinking feeling in his gut. He opened the throttle and raced to the end of the line.

As he jumped from the engine, early editions of the local newspaper were being dropped off on the platform. He tore open one of the bundles to get at one of the copies and read it by the dim gaslight of the rail yard. The banner headline hit him like a fist to the jaw:

TRAGEDY IN A COTTAGE

Engine Driver Kills His Wife—His

Child—and Himself.

The following day, Brierly was promoted to Robson's old position as lead engineer on the Midnight Express. Fate was playing a cruel trick on him, indeed.

Brierly took over Robson's train the very next night. Onboard was the fireman who had served under Robson on those midnight runs for many years, ever since Brierly himself had been promoted to driver. As the express train rounded the bend near the Robson cottage that evening, Brierly could scarcely look out into the blackness. As if by some automated instinct, he pulled the train's whistle as he'd done in that spot countless times before. Hot tears welled in his eyes. He looked back at the fireman, who had removed his cap and was wiping away tears of his own.

And so they did, day after day, week after week. Once while heading out into the dark of midnight, and again while returning in the faint light of dawn. Brierly pulled the whistle and cried silently, the fireman touched his cap. They never talked about it, or even spoke the Robson name again. One man simply paid tribute to the lost engineer, while the other kept silent memoriam to his murdered wife. The pair settled into the monotony that comes with routine.

Several months later, however, that routine took a frightening turn.

One night while approaching the bend near the cottage, Brierly slowed the train to one-quarter throttle, the maximum safe speed for negotiating the curve. He pushed the handle closed and looked out forlornly at the dark cottage, as was his habit. He was startled out of his quiet misery by the fireman, who was shouting above the train's din behind him. Brierly turned to see what was the matter. The fireman was bellowing incoherently and pointing at the throttle lever. The engineer was confused. But before the fireman's warnings could fully register, he felt it. The steady thrum of the engine building beneath his feet. The huge train was accelerating just as they approached the curve. Brierly looked at the handle and saw that it was being pulled open. The train was nearly to half-throttle.

Brierly snatched the handle and pushed it back down to one-quarter, but not without some effort. He had to push against some unseen force that was working against him. Brierly finally managed to overpower the mysterious energy that was fighting against him. The train went into the bend entirely too fast, wheels shrieking and sparking against the rails, but she stayed on the tracks.

"That was Jim's hand on the lever! I know it was!" shouted the fireman.

From that night on, the dangerous, haunted game was repeated over and over again. Every time the train came near the sweeping bend by the old Robson cottage, Brierly had to struggle mightily against some unseen force bent on forcing the throttle open and sending the cars and their passengers careening off the rails. Lately, it required more force than Brierly was able to muster on his own. So twice a day the strapping, square-jawed fireman had to put down his shovel and take his place alongside Brierly. The considerable force of the two men combined was just enough to counter the ghostly hand that pulled the throttle in the opposite direction.

Brierly was in a panic by the time he came to Cheiro with his story. The engineer told the mystic he wanted just two things: one was to hear that someone believed his story about the ghost at the throttle; the other was to have some authority on the subject, like Cheiro, go to the fireman and dismiss the whole thing as fantasy. Brierly told Cheiro that the very next day he was taking his wife and daughter on the Midnight Express with him. He was leaving London and the LMS company and retiring to a little cottage his family owned in the north of England. He had one more run to make and, for him, it would be finished. But he wanted the fireman to be able to go on unafraid.

"Come with me to the terminal tonight," Brierly begged Cheiro. "Tell the fireman my story is all nonsense. That it's something caused by overwrought nerves.

"Once I'm gone, I know Jim will no longer have a reason to seek revenge on that train," Brierly added.

Cheiro agreed to go. Still, he had no idea how he was going to be able to convince a man he'd never met that these supernatural experiences he'd been having for months in the presence of an equally frantic coworker were mere figments of the two men's imaginations. It was an especially difficult assignment, Cheiro thought, because he himself had come to believe that Brierly really had been dealing with a spirit from beyond the grave. Whether his shameful relationship with the dead man's wife was the cause of the haunting was anyone's guess, but it seemed fairly evident that the ghost of Jim Robson was, indeed, haunting the LMS Railway's Midnight Express.

When Cheiro arrived at the terminal that night, the Midnight Express was due to depart in less than an hour. The clairvoyant was introduced to Brierly's wife and five-year-old daughter, who were seated in an empty car closest to the engine. The wife was soft-spoken and kind, but with a sad expression of resignation in her eyes. He greeted the family politely, then made his way to the engine to meet the fireman.

Despite his intimidating size and obvious strength, the fireman was even more spooked by the ghostly encounters on the train than Brierly. Cheiro immediately sensed that telling this man his experiences were fantasy would be pointless. Instead, the clairvoyant started questioning the fireman.

"Have you actually seen the throttle lever move?" Cheiro asked.

"Seen it move? My God, yes!" the fireman shot back. "And I've felt it move. Only three nights ago we both had to hold the lever back with all of our strength or the train would have been dashed at 60 miles per hour around the bend and neither he nor I would be here to talk about it."

"Did you see anything else?" Cheiro asked.

"As clear as I see you standing in front of me now, I saw the shape of my old mate, Jim Robson, standing beside Brierly. Jim had his right hand gripping the throttle, as I've seen him do a thousand times.

Cheiro asked him if maybe the experience wasn't, perhaps, the product of nerves or of sadness over the loss of his friend Jim.

The big man towered over Cheiro. In his low rumble of a voice he said with a bit of dark humor, "Do I look to you like a man who sees ghosts?"

By now, the last of the evening's passengers were onboard and the whistle blew once, indicating the train would be departing shortly. Cheiro bade the fireman a safe trip, uncertain that he'd been able to help anyone at all. He poked his head into the first car to say goodnight to Brierly's wife and child. The wife was staring glumly out the window; the child was quiet, gently stroking the hair of her doll. He decided not to disturb them.

Brierly came aboard and shook Cheiro's hand. "Thank you, sir," the engineer said. "Thank you for coming."

Cheiro was the last to leave the platform as the third whistle blew, and Brierly set his hand to the throttle to start the train moving in a hiss of steam. Writing about the encounter years later, Cheiro said, "A presentiment of horror and tragedy gripped my very soul," as the train pulled away from the station. Back at home, Cheiro sat in his study contemplating the helplessness of mortals and the power of fate to take the helm when it pleases. He stared at the chair that Brierly had occupied earlier in the evening. Then the phone rang.

"Is your name Cheiro?" a voice asked. It was an area hospital attendant calling.

"I have a message for you from an employee on the Midnight Express. He was brought to us after a terrible accident on the train this evening. He wanted you to know that the engine and the first car jumped the tracks on a bend. The engineer, James Brierly, and his wife and daughter were killed. The fireman was thrown free and survived. He asks you to come to the hospital at once."

Chapter 9

The Soldier
and the Nun

When her beloved was ripped away from her, she took a vow to never love of this world again. But that was the least of the earthly misery for this poor, religious girl who still mopes about the corridors of a Pennsylvania Catholic school.

Rose looked up bashfully, scanning the row of boys lined up against the opposite wall of the big, old barn. This was supposed to be a dance, a mixer of sorts, but there was precious little dancing going on. Mostly the boys stayed huddled around a few loud-talking jokers, laughing it up while the girls whispered and giggled and occasionally smiled at them. In the middle of the hay-strewn floor, an old record player droned out Artie Shaw's "Begin the Beguine."

"What do you think of that tall boy there?" one of the girls asked Rose.

"I don't know," she answered. "He looks very gentle and kind of smart."

"Ugh!" the girl shouted. "Gentle and smart? You can tell all that from here? I think he's too skinny. And look at the suit he's wearing. How many older brothers do you suppose wore it before he finally got his chance at it?"

Several of the girls broke up laughing. They walked away, leaving Rose alone to stare at the floor and occasionally look across at the boys, who were doing their best not to look at anything at all. This dance was a terrible idea, Rose thought. Even on a normal school day, she felt awkward, out of place. What was she thinking, coming here? Lately, a lot of her time had been spent wondering just such things. What was she doing? Where was she going? What kind of life was right for a shy, thoughtful girl who much preferred books and poetry to party dresses and makeup?

She was at the top of her sophomore class at nearby Mercyhurst College, a Catholic girls' boarding school in Erie, Pennsylvania. There, Rose was right at home. She loved to walk Mercyhurst's manicured grounds, admiring the campus's stately Tudor buildings. Occasionally, she'd climb O'Neil Tower and look out toward Lake Erie and think that her life wouldn't be so bad if she never left Mercyhurst ever again. To her, it was a little bit of heaven on earth. Those feelings lately had her considering entering the school's convent, where she could chart a life on course to becoming a Sister of Mercy. Sister Rose. A nun. The life of quiet, contemplative solitude and service was increasingly appealing to her.

Surely, life in a nunnery couldn't be any worse than this barn dance, where now a half dozen of the boys had worked up enough nerve to pair up with girls and take to the center of the floor in some poor imitation of modern dance. Rose found watching the couples stumbling around in lopsided circles arm in arm particularly embarrassing. She decided it was time for her to get back to her dormitory room.

"Would you like to dance?"

Rose nearly jumped out of her skin. She hadn't seen the boy inching along the back wall of the barn. Even if she had, she wouldn't have expected him to talk to her, much less to ask her to dance. She looked at him for a full minute not knowing what to say, how to respond. It was the boy she'd seen across the room earlier, the skinny one with the threadbare, hand-me-down suit. Even up close, Rose thought, he looked gentle . . . and smart.

She stalled for time.

"I beg your pardon?" Rose feigned. "Would I like to what?"

"Dance," the boy said, motioning toward the center of the barn, which was filling up with couples emboldened by the courage of their peers. "Would you like to dance?" Then he added for emphasis, as if unsure himself, "With me."

Well, Rose thought, *he's made it pretty clear.* She couldn't pretend she hadn't heard or understood. She could be rude and simply turn away. Or she could reject him, sending him back to the other side of the barn, where he'd surely be mocked by the dwindling number of boys who remained alone there.

"Yes," Rose said.

"My name is Tom," the boy said, grinning and taking her arm, as if escorting her onto a luxury ocean liner. They walked to the center of the floor and fell into step with the rest of the couples, some of whom were now bravely augmenting their aimless circular shuffle with a few steps from the foxtrot.

"I'm Rose," she said and Tom put his hands on her waist.

"I know," Tom said. "I asked about you."

Few other words were spoken that evening. Tom and Rose danced every dance until the evening ended. By that time, Rose decided that she was right. Tom was really a nice, gentle boy. And she found that she liked being close to him. Holding him and being held by him. It felt right to her in a way she couldn't describe and certainly had never felt before. When they said goodnight, Rose felt a sharp, unfamiliar ache at their parting. She wanted to see him again.

So she was very pleased a few days later when one of the dorm supervisors came to her room and told her she had a visitor.

"Is it Tom?" Rose asked the messenger.

"I didn't ask," the woman replied. "It's a frightfully skinny boy with messy brown hair."

Rose's smile widened. "It's Tom."

Rose found Tom waiting for her downstairs, flowers in hand. He'd brought them, he said, because his brothers told him that's what a boy should do if he felt a girl was particularly special.

"Is that how you feel?" Rose asked.

"Oh, yes! Yes I do!" Tom replied.

From that moment on, the two were inseparable. Though Tom was a Protestant and not a college student, Rose's Catholic parents could see in him much of what their daughter saw. He was a good young man, gentle in nature and quite intelligent. Before long, Tom presented Rose with a simple gold ring, a symbol of their engagement. It was early winter 1941. Their families began to plan a wedding for the spring of 1942, a wedding that would never take place.

In December 1941, the drumbeat of global war reached a thunderous crescendo in the skies of Pearl Harbor in Hawaii. Suddenly the United States was pulled into World War II and across the nation, young men were drafted to fight the war on several fronts. Tom knew he had to go and serve his nation. His brothers were all going, as were nearly all of his friends.

"Let's marry before you leave," Rose said.

"Rose, we have no money, and besides there's no time," Tom replied.

"We don't need much," she said. "We'll have a simple wedding, just you and me. Please, Tom."

He held her close, her face cupped gently in his hands.

"Rose, I love you. Nothing in the world is going to keep us from being married and living the rest of our lives together. But I want to do it right. You deserve the best there is. And I want our children someday to know their dad did the right thing for his country when duty called. Let's wait, my love. When I return we'll have a wedding like you've only dreamed of."

Rose uneasily conceded. Tom was right. Now was not the time to rush through a marriage. He would go off to war and she would finish school. Everything would turn out all right. It would seem like forever, but she could wait. For the man she loved she could wait forever.

Tom was assigned to the army infantry. Within weeks he was shipped out to fight the Nazis in Europe. He wrote home regularly, telling Rose about the horrors of war and professing his ever deepening love for her.

"I don't think any of this would be remotely tolerable, if not for the knowledge of your love waiting for me at home," Tom wrote. "You sustain me, Rose. Pray for me and I will be home soon."

Rose found the letters heartbreaking. The thought of the kind, gentle boy she knew being hardened into manhood by war and violence both sickened and saddened her. But with her abundant faith she resolved to keep the love he relied on burning strong. She prayed for him almost constantly.

Early in the spring of 1942, Tom's correspondence stopped without warning. Rose was frantic. Her grades were suffering as she spent countless sleepless nights wondering what had happened to him. Finally, just one week before the spring day they had originally set for their wedding, a government official arrived at Tom's family home. They called

Rose to join them a short time later. Tom's father delivered the awful news.

"Rose, Tom has been killed in action," the old man told her, "along with his entire squad. Dead. All of them. Their bodies were never recovered."

Her head swam. This couldn't be happening. This was the man she loved. The man she never thought she'd find. They were going to be married. What was the matter with these people? He couldn't be dead. He was coming home to marry her. Why were they telling her this?

As if she had been physically kicked, Rose doubled over and fell to the floor in the kitchen of the simple farmhouse where Tom's family had already begun mourning his loss. The life she knew, and the life she had dreamed of were over.

Someone of lesser conviction might have turned against her religion in the face of such adversity. But Rose was a young woman of formidable faith. In the weeks and months that followed the tragic news, Rose found comfort in the Queens chapel at Mercyhurst. She spent long hours there in the shadowy, deep-blue room, lighting candles to Tom's memory and praying for guidance. Finally, she decided that she knew what she was to do with her life. Without a second thought, Rose stopped mourning her fiancé and joined the Sisters of Mercy. She would never love another man, she decided. She would become a nun after all.

Rose's training for her final vows was a study in dedication. Rose gave herself over fully to the task of serving the Church. When she finally took her vows of chastity, poverty, and obedience, she did so without hesitation or doubt. After the ceremony, she went alone into the chapel to pray. Symbolic of her transition from Tom's fiancée to bride of Christ, she took off her engagement ring for the first time since it had been given to her years before. She placed it on the tiny fingers of the Christ child statue and left it there. She had no more use for it.

Over the next few years, Sister Rose worked hard and became a trusted and valued member of the order. Most around her knew of her hardship and lost love, but it was never spoken of again. The young girl did a masterful job of using the tragedy to steel herself to life's challenges. It also made her especially sympathetic to the war widows who sought comfort and counsel from the Sisters of Mercy. Her life might have continued much the same way, a life of quiet prayer and dedicated service, if not for the discovery that the greatest tragedy Rose had ever known had all been a lie.

Just after noontime on an autumn day in 1945, Rose was heading from lunch to her afternoon prayers when the mother superior stopped Rose in the hallway. It was highly unusual for a nun to receive guests at Mercyhurst. It was even more unusual for the mother superior to announce the arrival of such a guest herself. *This must be very important,* Rose thought. *Perhaps the bishop is here, but what would the bishop want with me?*

"Wait in the chapel, Sister Rose," the mother superior directed. "We'll send your visitor in."

Rose sat in the pew and waited. She was curious and a little excited at this deviation from the normal day in the life of a Mercyhurst nun. Suddenly the side doors opened. From within the dark chapel, Rose could see only a lone silhouette against the blinding midday sun streaming in from outside. And yet, almost immediately she recognized Tom. He was in uniform. Still painfully thin, as always. But more important, very much alive. He ran to her and tried to embrace her. Her years of chastity in the habit forced her to keep him at arm's length.

"Rose, it's me!" Tom said.

"Oh my, Tom, I know," Rose stammered. "I'm so happy to see you, but what . . . why . . . ? They said you were . . ."

"Dead. Yes, I know. I'm so sorry, Rose. I'm so sorry so many people were hurt, but you most of all."

Tom tried to explain the unexplainable. How he'd come back from the dead four years after heading off to war. It started when his commanders really believed he and his squad were killed in an ambush in the run-up to the second battle at El Alamein. They hastily dispatched veteran's affairs officers with condolences for Tom's family and eleven other men. By the time the army realized that the men had not been killed, but rather had escaped the ambush and hidden behind enemy lines for more than a month, the memorial services at home were long over.

"Why didn't they tell us then, Tom?" Rose whispered. The pain of those days and months was rushing back to her. She started to cry. "Why couldn't they just say they made a mistake and that you were alive?"

"It's because of what we did in that month we were missing," Tom said. "If the army had ever let on that any of us had lived, a great many men might have died."

Tom spent the rest of the afternoon telling Rose how they'd lived as fugitives behind German lines, working to hide and stay alive, but also collecting enormous amounts of intelligence. Troop numbers, movements, equipment schedules. His squad, quite by accident, became some of the best informed spies in the entire Allied war effort. When they finally made it back to their unit and were debriefed, the army decided it couldn't risk letting the Germans know that

Allied soldiers had survived for so long so close to their operations. The men were forbidden from communicating with family until the war ended.

"We took an oath," Tom said. "We did it for our country. Oh, Rose, but I'm home now. All these years I kept the flame of our love burning bright inside of me. Tell me you can leave this convent and be my wife at last."

Rose felt a sickly feeling building inside of her. Of course she was thrilled beyond words that Tom was home safe. She loved this man deeply. There was a time when her life seemed perfectly worthless without him. But that time had passed. She was committed to her work with the Sisters of Mercy now. How could she turn her back on the promises she'd made to the order and to God himself?

"I've taken an oath myself, you know," she told Tom quietly. She took him gently by the hand and led him to the statue of the Christ child. She pointed to the tiny, delicate porcelain hand.

Tom immediately recognized the engagement ring he'd given Rose four years before. He started to cry. This was not the homecoming he'd dreamed of as he gritted out endless days and nights of war. Somewhere outside, bells began to toll.

"I must go now, Tom."

"I understand," he lied. He put his uniform cap back on and tried to stride out of the chapel with as much dignity as he could. He tried hard to stifle the sobs that were wracking his body from within.

A few days after Tom returned, his family and Rose's joined forces to try to convince the young nun to leave the convent and return to a normal life as a wife to the man who loved her so deeply. She told them the truth.

She would meditate and pray about the matter, seeking spiritual guidance. She belonged to God now. In the end, it was His decision.

There would be no easy answer from on high. The more Rose sequestered herself in the dark chapel, the more conflicted she became. She prayed and wept before the statue of the Christ child, but all she felt in return was that she was being pulled apart by two great forces bent on destroying her. What had she done that was so wrong? she demanded. Why was she being tortured for following a pure heart from tragic love lost to a life of godly service?

With what seemed like nothing but a life of conflict and sadness ahead of her, Rose fell into a deep depression. A short time later she did the only thing she could think of to ease the pain. In her tiny, sparsely appointed room directly above the Queens chapel at Mercyhurst, Sister Rose tied a blanket to a ceiling light fixture and hanged herself.

News of her suicide rocked the Sisters of Mercy and the college at large. It didn't take long before reports began of apparitions of the young nun all around the campus, especially around the college tower and in the Queens chapel and nearby Christ the King cathedral. Witnesses saw her wandering the grounds as if looking for something. She appeared in students' rooms, often reflected in mirrors or passing like a misty vapor through the dormitory halls.

Sister Rose's ghost remained mostly benign until a female student crossed paths with it in a violent way.

Lori was a senior in 1954. She was looking forward to graduation, but, more than that, she was anxious to marry the love of her life, a student at the nearby state college in Erie. The two had been dating for nearly four years. Time enough, Lori thought, for her boyfriend to step up and make their engagement official. She decided a little practical joke was in order.

Lori called her boyfriend and asked him to meet her on a Wednesday evening at the Mercyhurst campus.

"Why?" he asked. "We see each other every weekend. I have a lot of schoolwork to do. Can't this wait until Saturday?"

"It cannot wait until Saturday," Lori said with mock seriousness. She tried desperately not to laugh to avoid spoiling the joke. "I have a very urgent matter that I need to discuss with you. It concerns my future as well as yours. Please be here."

With that, she hung up. Lori snuck down to the darkened chapel and felt her way along in the faint candlelight to the statue of the Christ child. Her heart was racing from both excitement and fear as she reached up and snatched Sister Rose's engagement ring off the statue's tiny finger. As soon as she had it in her hand, a blast of cold wind shot through the chapel, extinguishing the candles and leaving her in pitch blackness. She gasped and the sound echoed around the cavernous room. Slowly, as she felt her way along the wall and the floor, inching her way to the door, a frightening thought crossed Lori's mind. What if it was locked? What if she were trapped in here in the blackness with the ring from a dead nun in her hand? She felt panic welling up inside.

She grabbed for the door latch and pushed the door with all of her might. It was open. She went sprawling out onto the sidewalk in a heap. She examined her hands and legs. A few incidental scratches but nothing more. That's when she noticed that she still had a death grip on the ring, which was digging a raw, red furrow into her palm.

Lori's plan was simple, if a bit childish. She was going to wear Sister Rose's ring and pretend she'd been asked by another boy to be his bride. She hoped the cruel gag would make her boyfriend see the wisdom in asking for her hand right away. She tried the ring on. It fit perfectly. But as she sat there admiring the gold band glinting in the faint chapel light, all at once a wave of sadness washed over her.

"Oh, Sister Rose," she whispered aloud. "You poor, poor thing."

Like most Mercyhurst students, she knew the tragic story of the young nun. How horrible it would be to find your one true love, only to think him lost forever. Recalling the awful story of Sister Rose gave her pause. For a moment, she had second thoughts about her little joke. But it was a harmless prank, she thought. Besides, Sister Rose might appreciate taking part in bringing two young lovers together.

Lori was quite wrong.

As she waited outside her dormitory for her boyfriend that Wednesday evening, she heard a shrieking coming from inside the building. One of her roommates raced outside and, without words, embraced her.

"What is the matter with you?" Lori asked, pushing the now crying student off of her. "Are you crazy? What's going on?"

"Lori, the police just called here looking for you," the girl said. "They are coming here to talk to you now."

"Talk to me? Why in the world do the police want to talk to me?" She began to fidget with the ring on her finger. Could someone have found out she'd taken it? Could she be accused of theft? She never meant to keep it. Surely she could explain that.

"It's your boyfriend, Lori," the hysterical student finally said. "He was coming here to meet you when a truck crossed in front of him and hit his car. They said he's dead, Lori. I'm so sorry. He's dead."

Lori was crushed. She ran straight back to the chapel and put the ring back on the statue of the Christ child. Then she fell to the floor of the chapel and wept bitterly well into the night. She was found on the floor of the chapel the next morning, exhausted and incoherent.

"The ring did it," she kept repeating. "The ring killed him."

Word spread quickly about the incident and, while Mercyhurst officials were loath to attribute the accidental death of a state college student to a haunted ring in their chapel, they decided nonetheless to remove the ring from the statue and keep it locked up with the institution's other valuables. Rose had other ideas for it, however. Whenever the ring was kept out of sight, encounters with Sister Rose's ghost increased. Those sightings would inevitably be followed by the mysterious return of the ring from the university safe to the finger of the Christ child in the Queens chapel.

After a half dozen attempts to keep the ring under lock and key, Mercyhurst administrators decided that burying it might better serve all involved. The location of the ring's final interment has never been made public. But shortly after the decision was made, a curious, oval grass island was built in the lot between Mercyhurst's Weber Hall and the entrance to the Queens chapel. Students discovered quickly that stepping over the grass mound, rather than walking around it, was a sure way to fail a test, be cut from a sports team, or lose a boyfriend or girlfriend. The tiny plot, whether or not it hides Sister Rose's cursed engagement ring, is evidently brimming with bad luck.

As for the spirit of Sister Rose, she continues to haunt the Catholic school, appearing more frequently to young women and young lovers. Countless paranormal investigators have examined the college and the convent, some coming away with what they say is definitive proof—audio recordings, photographs, videos—of Sister Rose's presence. In response to all of the attention an active haunting can bring, Mercyhurst officials have since taken to locking the chapel and the Old Main tower at 10 p.m., perhaps to keep the curious out, or perhaps to keep the lovesick nun in.

Chapter 10
The Road
between Lovers

The young couple thought they could convince the world of their true love. But not even the ultimate sacrifice could soften their families' hearts, leaving the two young lovers to continue forever their sad, futile attempt at being together.

It was, perhaps, the last chance Elisha and Jemima had to salvage their young love. Elisha packed a few last items in a carpetbag and looked down the gravel carriage road that ran through the west yard of his family's property. He was leaving this home in Tolland, Connecticut, to fight in the Revolution. So far, the year of 1775 had not been kind to the Benton family. Already two of his brothers had died after being captured by the British. But it was something Elisha had to do, for his young country, and, not less important, because he believed the time away from home would soften the hearts of Jemima's family, which had forbidden the couple to wed despite their insistence that they loved each other deeply.

"You'll be careful, won't you?" Jemima said.

Poor girl, Elisha thought. She was more than twelve years younger than he. Still a child really. He loved her so much. But could she really understand what he was doing, where he was going?

"I'll be as careful as any man at war can be," he told her, kissing her forehead and brushing away one fat tear from her cheek with his thumb. "Tell your mother and father I said goodbye. Tell them I hope that while I'm away, the Barrows family will soften their hearts and let their daughter marry the man who loves her more than anything."

"Oh, Elisha. I'll be right here waiting. No matter how long, I'll be waiting for you."

He allowed himself the luxury of one final embrace, lingering in her arms there in the shadow of the house his grandfather Daniel Benton had built with his own hands in 1720. Then he drew in a deep breath, hoisted his bag, and started with purpose down the dirt road.

"I love you, Elisha Benton," Jemima called after him. He dared not turn around and let her see the tears streaming down his face. He lifted one hand to his cap and bade her a last goodbye with his back turned toward her. And then he was gone. Jemima walked dejectedly the quarter mile back to her home, where she spent the ensuing months barely eating or drinking, in a constant vigil for the man she loved but could not have.

The war for independence took a harsh toll on the colonial residents of northwest Connecticut and western Massachusetts that year. Within a year of his leaving, the bluecoat regiment to which Elisha had been assigned was overrun by the British. Jemima was alone in her room when word reached Tolland that the last of the Benton boys had been taken to a filthy, disease-ridden redcoat prison ship anchored in the harbor of New York. Jemima's mother knocked gently on her daughter's door.

"Jemmy, are you awake?" Mrs. Barrows called into the darkened room.

"I am, Mother. What is it?"

"Jemmy, dear, there's news about the Benton boy."

Jemima perked up. She rose and sat at the edge of her bed.

"What is it, Mother? Tell me. Has he come home from the war already?"

"No, dear. I'm sorry," her mother said. Then she paused. As sure as she was that her daughter should not have been allowed to marry Elisha Benton, a young man nearly twice Jemima's age, she could hardly bring herself to tell the young girl the wretched news. She couldn't bear to break her daughter's heart again. Still, the girl deserved to know the truth.

"Tell me, Mother!" Jemima demanded.

"Elisha was taken captive by the British soldiers, just like his brothers," Mrs. Barrows finally said. "They took him to the prison ships. Very few of the men make it out of there alive, Jemmy. Two Benton boys are dead already. I fear for Mrs. Benton that she's soon to bury her third and final son."

"He's still alive, then?" Jemima asked with unusual gaiety.

"Well, yes. Yes, he is. For now. He's alive and a prisoner of the British Crown."

"Then I know he'll be just fine, Mother. You'll see. He'll be home soon and he'll be just fine."

It was enough talk for one afternoon, Mrs. Barrows thought. Why torture the poor girl any further? Let her believe her young soldier would come marching home none the worse for his adventures. What could it hurt? Her love was the fancy of a young girl, smitten with a boy she barely knew, the old woman thought. It was nothing real. It was nothing lasting. She could love him right up until the day they buried him. A day that would come soon enough, Mrs. Barrows thought.

Elisha spent every painful, waking moment praying for just one last glimpse of Jemima. His leg had been badly damaged during the ambush that led to his capture. Infection had set in and the pain was so unbearable, it was difficult to remain conscious. But in his few brief moments of lucidity, he prayed.

"If I can just see her one more time, Lord. Just for a moment. Just to say goodbye and to tell her my love never waned. Then you can take me. Thy will be done."

Elisha's injuries were but a small part of his problems aboard the dingy prison ship. Men howled with pain and were wracked with coughing from morning until night. It was well known among the prisoners that deadly, contagious diseases were sweeping through the reeking boat, decimating the ranks of the incarcerated. Late at night, the American rebels whispered that the British were exposing the prisoners on purpose, handing out infected blankets and eating utensils in an effort to thin the ranks on the ship.

A month into his confinement, Elisha had resigned himself to dying aboard the prison ship. He was delirious from fever and wracked with chills. And his arms and legs had begun to show the creeping raised bumps that marked the telltale first stages of smallpox.

"If I could just see Jemima one more time," he prayed.

And out of nowhere, his prayers were answered.

A British officer came down into the hold of the ship and picked out twelve prisoners seemingly at random. Elisha Benton was one of them. The men were led above to the main deck, where Elisha saw what he could only imagine was a hallucination brought on by his fever. A company of colonial soldiers stood onboard the prison ship. A group of sickly looking redcoats cowered in front of them, being kept in check by the rebel bayonets.

A British officer turned to Elisha's group.

"This is the luckiest day in your miserable lives," the officer told them "You men are part of a prisoner exchange. That you dogs are being valued equally, man for man, with fine, loyal soldiers who serve the king with honor is none of my doing, I can assure you."

The officer stared at Elisha, who was nearly doubled over with fatigue and pain.

"Go now. Go with these other rebel cur. Be gone, and remember the benevolence of the royal Crown."

Before Elisha could fully fathom what was going on, he was being led by fellow American soldiers away from the ship, away from New York and back to Connecticut, where, with what little time he had left, he could see his family.

Word reached the Benton household before Elisha arrived. The family was told their only living son was deathly ill with smallpox. He would almost certainly die. In the meantime, he would need constant care from someone who would have to be very close to a dying man with a virulently contagious illness.

"Has anyone here ever survived smallpox?" the messenger asked.

"Well, no. Why?" Elisha's mother asked.

"Having a mild case of the pox gives one immunity to the disease. You'll need to find someone who has built a tolerance for it," he said. "Or someone foolish enough to risk getting it themselves."

The family looked around among themselves, unsure of what to do.

"Perhaps it's best we take him to an army facility, then?" the messenger asked. "They have trained people there who can care for him until he passes."

The Bentons were stunned. Silent.

"I'll do it."

None of them had seen Jemima Barrows walking slowly up the carriage road. She'd been listening the entire time.

"Bring him here. I'll take care of him."

"But my dear, have you ever had the pox?" Mrs. Benton asked.

"Never," the young girl replied firmly. "It matters not. I want to do it. We've tried to tell all of you that Elisha and I are in love. I know of no better way to demonstrate this to you. All that matters is that from this day forward, nobody will ever doubt our love again."

With few other choices, the Benton family agreed that Elisha would be brought home to be cared for by Jemima. Because they feared the dread disease that was killing their son, he had be kept in a room at the far end of an addition that stretched to the rear of the Benton homestead like a giant L. When he first arrived, the soldiers carried Elisha to his deathbed and tried to make him as comfortable as they could. Jemima walked in as they were saying their goodbyes.

"You're a brave young woman," one of the soldiers said to Jemima, tipping his cap.

"Thank you for bringing him here safely, gentlemen. You've done a great service for him and for me. He is in good hands now. Go with God."

The soldiers left. Jemima slowly approached the bed. She looked down at Elisha, so frail and gaunt. His face was the color of wet ashes. Tears filled her eyes, but her heart was still so full of love for him. She brushed the matted hair off of his forehead with her fingers. His eyes opened and he saw her face for the first time since he'd turned and walked away from her down the carriage road months before.

"Jemima, my love," he whispered. "I prayed so hard to see you."

"Shhh. I know you did," she answered. "As did I. Our prayers are answered, Elisha. I am going to take care of you. You are going to get well."

While Jemima relished Elisha's homecoming, the rest of the area families viewed the sick young man's presence with grave concern. The local cemetery had been filled to capacity with Tolland residents who had been killed by smallpox. Everyone around the Benton place knew what a danger the disease, and anyone with it, posed to the neighborhood. Folks began to give the Benton homestead a wide berth. And they stayed well away from the room out back where Elisha lay dying under the attentive care of one very dedicated lovestruck teen girl. The two were shut away together. Food and provisions were lowered through a skylight, but except for that brief contact with the outside world, Jemima saw only Elisha. It was all she wanted.

Fall turned to winter. Jemima spent Christmas locked in the room with her beloved. He never improved. The disease ran rampant through his weakened body. In the last days he simply lay, shivering, in the arms of the girl who adored him, the girl he loved but could not marry. Finally, mercifully, the end came on January 22, 1777. When the men opened the skylight to lower the week's rations, they saw

Jemima huddled in a corner, sobbing into her hands. The sheets of the bed had been pulled up to cover Elisha's body fully. The men quietly closed the skylight and got down from the roof to spread the sad news.

From inside the dying room, Jemima heard the church bell ringing. *Everyone knows now,* she thought. *There will be a funeral soon. And soon after that, another.* She pulled up the sleeve of her dress to scratch at the bumpy, scabby rash that was spreading over her body.

The Bentons were so fearful of the pox that they wouldn't have their son's body moved through the house, for fear of contamination. Instead, his body was passed through a window directly into the undertaker's carriage, which clattered off noisily down the gravel road to where the body would be prepared. The casket was brought back to the Benton house later that evening, where a funeral was held in the family parlor.

Elisha's burial took place just steps from the room where he'd died. A small, flat headstone marked his grave on the north side of the carriage road that split the Benton property in two. It was very near the spot where Elisha had said goodbye to Jemima as he headed off to war. Jemima could not attend the funeral, as she was already deathly ill with the smallpox she'd contracted while nursing Elisha. She simply waited, alone, in the room at the back of the Benton house. She waited to die. She was not afraid at all. She was eager to join her lover in the next life, having been denied the chance to celebrate their love in this one.

Jemima was found dead on the morning of February 28, 1777. She was seventeen years old. Beside her body was a note asking only that she be buried with her love, Elisha. It was a request that would not be kept.

Because of her incredible sacrifice in caring for their son, the Benton family paid all of Jemima Barrows's funeral expenses and agreed to have her buried on the Benton property. But as she and Elisha were never married, it would be inappropriate for the two to be buried side by side. Jemima, they decided, would be buried on the south side of the carriage road. In death, as in life, Elisha and Jemima were near each other, but still kept apart by the will of their families.

Stories of the unexplained around the Benton homestead began almost immediately after Jemima's death. And they have never ceased. Benton family ancestors lived in the house for more than 150 years after Jemima and Elisha were buried there. Throughout that time, family members and visitors became accustomed to the sound of a woman crying. The warped floors, crooked walls, and tiny doorways of the ancient New England house all seemed to hide some fleeting shadow of the weeping woman. Dozens of people heard the sound over the years, but no source could ever be found. Throughout the nineteenth century, the Benton homestead's reputation as a haunted house grew throughout Tolland. Those who chanced pass by the house on winter nights often saw the misty, glowing vision of a woman in what appeared to be a wedding dress, wandering the frozen grounds and weeping as if searching for something.

Despite the morbid past and chilling reputation of the Benton property, Florrie Bishop Bowering fell in love with the place the first time she saw it. The blood-red clapboard, the moldy shake roof, the brick and flagstone foundation, even the ramshackle picket fence were quintessential New

England, Florrie thought. With the money she'd made as a radio star in Hartford, she could afford most anything she wanted. In 1932, she bought the Benton homestead. She'd be the first person outside the Benton family to live there since Daniel Benton set the first foundation stone in 1720.

She may have been an outsider, but Florrie lovingly cared for the property as if she were a Benton herself. For the next thirty-seven years, she, her loyal maid, and a handyman poured their hearts into restoring the place to its original, colonial-era grandeur. She shared her work with thousands of guests who attended numerous, lavish affairs on the property over the years. And while she knew the stories of Elisha's death and Jemima's ghost, she never encountered anything supernatural in all of her time there.

But she knew it was real. Her maid told her constantly of the weeping she heard in every part of the house. Overnight guests were often disturbed by the same pitiful and mysterious sounds. Still, Florrie loved the old place, ghosts and all. It was with some reluctance that, in 1969, she decided the big old property was more than she could manage; she deeded the place over to the Tolland Historical Society. Ever since, the society's officials, guides, and volunteers have been stewards of the storied property, as well as regular witnesses to the persistent supernatural activity there. Nearly all of it, they say, is attributed to the ghost of Jemima Barrows.

In addition to the visions of a ghostly woman and the sounds of her crying, those who tour the old Benton place have reported mysterious "vibrations," uncomfortable sensations that left them shaken and afraid, though nothing was ever seen or heard. One of the historical society's volunteers once snuck upstairs to the second floor of the house, an area normally off limits to both visitors and staff. She skipped up the stairs nonchalantly, but she came down slowly, quietly. Her face had gone deathly pale.

"There were vibrations up there," she stammered to a friend. "I never want to go there again."

Charles Marsden was feeling exactly those kinds of vibrations when he stopped to photograph the Benton homestead in the fall of 1983. He'd driven about a half hour down State Road 32 from his house in Belchertown, Massachusetts, looking for historic old Cape-style houses from which he could draw ideas on how to renovate his own colonial-era property. He'd already stopped at a dozen homes, snapping pictures in places with names like Dingley Dell, Cotton Hollow, Stafford Springs, and Little Rest. By the time he pulled into Tolland, he figured he had enough pictures and plenty of inspiration for his renovation project. Besides, it was getting late and would be dusk soon enough. Still, something made him continue down Metcalf Road.

When he came upon the Benton house, Charles ground his car to a halt on the gravel shoulder of the road and stared at the place, dumbstruck. It was as if he'd had a vision of this very place when he'd first set out to fix up the eighteenth-century home he'd inherited the year before. In all of the sketches he'd done, in all of the plans he'd drawn up, this was exactly how he imagined his own home, right down to the blood-red walls and powder-blue doors. He was having an overwhelming sense of déjà vu. This place was like something he'd seen in a dream. It felt at once familiar and disquieting. Still, it was exactly the kind of house he was looking for when he set off on this little jaunt. He grabbed his camera and hopped out of the car, anxious to get a few photographs of the exterior in the waning autumn daylight. The setting sun cast a warm orange glow on everything around the Benton house that wasn't already covered by the long afternoon shadows.

He leveled his beat-up Pentax K-1000 at the house, but before he could bring the image into focus, he noticed the needle on the light meter waving wildly from top to bottom in the viewfinder. He banged the body of the camera against his palm. *Maybe the battery is going dead,* he thought. He brought the viewfinder back to his eye and saw that the needle was pinned up beyond the overexposure mark. It was as if he were pointing the lens directly into the sun. Except that he was aimed squarely into the shadowy area on the northeast side of the Benton house. He twisted the lens to bring the building into focus. He could now see the blurred image of a window. It was glowing, bathed in an eerie, otherworldly bluish light. The light was spilling out from inside the empty house. He sharpened the focus and froze in his tracks. There was a woman in the window staring back at him.

She was young and radiated a sadness Charles could feel even out here in the yard. As he stared at her through the camera lens, awestruck, he could see that she was crying. More than that, he could hear it, a faraway sound of sobbing as if in a dream or emanating from an endless tunnel. By instinct, he fired the shutter and that's when he felt the vibration. It was like a raw, electrical current coursing through him. It wasn't painful. But it was profoundly disturbing. With his naked eye he looked at the window, which was now nothing but a blind, dark hole in an empty building. He had no more desire to explore the old Benton place. He hurried back to his car, the sound of the crying still ringing in his ears, the vibrations still chilling him to the bone. As he drove away, he watched the Benton homestead disappear into his rearview mirror, half expecting to see the ghostly woman, but seeing only the Tolland woods at sunset.

It was several days before he gathered the nerve to develop the black-and-white film. He scanned the negative of his lone shot of the Benton house. It seemed unremarkable. He took the film into the darkroom to make a print of the photo. He feared to look as the image came to life in the pan of developer, but there was no odd glow; there was no face of a weeping young girl. There was, however, a reflection. The angle, the old leaded window glass, and the low afternoon light combined to create a crystal-clear reflection of one area of the Benton place's west yard. In the window, Charles could see two identical areas of flattened dirt under flat fieldstone markers, one on either side of the carriage road on which he was standing when he took the picture.

By aiming at the house, Charles Marsden had made the perfect picture of the simple, but hardly final, resting places of Elisha Benton and Jemima Barrows.

Chapter 11

The Fisherman's Wife of Red Moon Island

On a sandy island thirty miles off the coast of South Korea stands a cryptic stone monument of a grieving bride. Not far from the statue, visitors to this remote place often find the ghost of the young widow herself, still searching the beach for her lost love.

She was on her knees, thin brown fingers sifting through the gold, sugary sand of Janggol Beach, when she saw him. It was just as she'd seen him countless times before. He always walked several steps behind his father, dragging a bait bucket and wrestling with a patchwork sail wrapped around a mast that was twice his height. She smiled and sat back on her heels to watch them.

Like every other father and son on the tiny island of Jawoldo, the island of the red moon, they were heading to their boat for a long day of fishing for snapper, eel, and crab. Fish were the lifeblood of this little windswept place, its reason for being. The day's haul would be brought to the bustling street markets across the harbor in the Korean port city of Incheon, where it would be sold, traded, bartered—adding one more day to the island's fragile economy. As a result, Jawoldo girls were granted a fair bit of time to enjoy their childhoods. The boys were cast to the sea—as they'd been for countless generations—at a very tender age.

She always watched him, this boy. He was a fisherman. And someday she'd be a fisherman's wife. It wasn't some romantic notion sprung from watching him plod up toward the brightly painted wooden boat day after day. It was a simple fact. That's what girls in Jawoldo became. As sure as the boys took to the waves. Lately, she'd begun to wonder if, just maybe, she could be this particular young fisherman's wife.

She still remembered how, as little children, toddlers really, they had played together on the dusty clay steps that separated her family's home from his. They'd played that way until her young-girl interests took her elsewhere and his life started heading toward the sea. Since then, they'd made polite gestures in passing and little more. Still, she remembered their time together. He'd been quiet then. Too soft and gentle for a life of hauling hand lines and killing fish and withering in the sun out there on the Yellow Sea, she thought now. Yet here he was, already showing the chiseled brown shoulders and faraway squint that defined all of the men she'd ever known.

So today she ran to him, floating gracefully over the powdery sand until she caught up to the boy and his father.

"Hello, Chin-ho." Her voice was strong, clear even above the wind and the steady churn of the surf, the run up the beach apparently effortless.

The boy's father looked back over his shoulder and grunted, quickly turning his attention back toward his destination down near the waterline. The boy beamed when he saw her. He straightened up and held the sail mast high over one shoulder.

"Hi, Chung-ae!" the boy shouted. "What are you doing out here?"

"I'm picking shells for my mother and sister. They're busy making lanterns for the fall festival. They need these tiny trumpet shells to decorate them." She drew close to him and held out her hand. A few perfectly formed miniature shells. He brushed them around her palm with his finger, admiring them.

"Seems like I'm the only one who can find them." She smiled, proud of herself.

"Will you be making lanterns, too?" Chin-ho asked.

"Oh, yes! My sister is teaching me. We're making a great dragon with scales and horns and flaming wings to cover the path in front of our house. You should see it!"

"I'd like to see it when I get back," he said. "We'll be out all night fishing, but I'll be back tomorrow morning. Will you show me then?"

Chung-ae smiled, blushing. "I'll wait here on the beach for you. Then we can go see!"

"I'll see you tomorrow," Chin-ho said, now hurrying to catch up to his father, who was looking back with annoyance as he neared the boat. "Goodbye, Chung-ae."

She stayed there in the same spot, pretending to look for shells as she watched Chin-ho and his father load their boat and shove off from the shore into the rolling waves. She looked at the place in the sand where he'd dug an ankle-deep hole while shuffling his feet nervously when he spoke to her. She walked over and stood in that spot, her tiny feet in his footprints, and watched Chin-ho's boat sail out of sight.

The next day, she was on the beach before dawn, scanning the dark western horizon, looking for the little patchwork sail. The morning sky was just going from dusty orange to the harsh light of day when she saw them returning. She ran down to the flat, wet sand where waves lapped Janggol Beach. She waved both arms above her head. From the bow of the boat, she saw Chin-ho waving back. As young as she was, she felt some oddly familiar thrill at the sight of him; a thrill born of a hundred generations of Jawoldo women waiting for the sea to return their men. *This is what it feels like to be a fisherman's wife,* Chung-ae thought. *This is what it would feel like to be this particular fisherman's wife.* She liked the way it felt.

When he'd secured the boat and helped his father load their catch onto a market cart, he walked to where Chung-ae was standing.

"I don't smell very good," he warned her as he approached.

"I don't care," she lied.

They walked in happy silence to her family's house, where she showed him all the things she'd made for Chusuk, the fall festival. Her mother came out and saw the boy patiently reviewing Chung-ae's handiwork. The mother brought the boy sweet rice cakes and a barley tea, a wordless expression of gratitude for his kindness. When Chusuk arrived, the mother invited the boy's family to join them in the celebration, which lasted all day and all night. The men drank and sang, the women gossiped and giggled, and Chung-ae and Chin-ho sat together watching the lanterns dance in the ocean breeze against a sky filled with fireworks and a full harvest moon.

Months later, there was a knock on the door at Chung-ae's house. The mother answered and was greeted by a well-known matchmaker from the nearby island of Yeongheongdo.

"Mrs. Pak, I have come to talk to you about your daughter, Chung-ae. She is nearing the age for marriage, and I have a good young man from a fine family on my island who would like to discuss arranging an engagement."

From the shadows inside the house, Chung-ae could hear what the man was saying. It was not a surprise. She knew this day would come. Marriages were contracts between families. They were arranged according to the realities of economics, not the affairs of the heart. Just as she'd always expected, her mother was now discussing her wedding to a man she'd never met or heard of before. But suddenly, Chung-ae heard something she could not believe. She strained to hear, in case she had misunderstood what her mother had just told the matchmaker.

"I'm sorry, Mrs. Pak, what did you say?" the matchmaker asked.

"I said my daughter is already engaged, sir," the mother said. "Yes, it is all arranged. She is to marry Lee Chin-ho, a boy from our own village."

The matchmaker apologized for the misunderstanding and promptly left. In the house, Chung-ae's heart leapt at her mother's words. But how was this possible? Nothing had been said about her marrying Chin-ho. She ran to her mother, who was staring blankly out the kitchen window.

"Umma, what's wrong?"

"Nothing," the old woman replied. "Why don't you go bring your father some tea."

"Umma, I heard what you said. You said I was going to marry Chin-ho."

The mother turned to look at her daughter. The old woman's face was ashen, her eyes filling with tears. "I lied," she said.

"But why, Umma?"

"Because I've watched the two of you together for many years, Chung-ae. You've grown from children together and now there is love between you. You were meant to be with him. You were meant to be Chin-ho's wife. Now I must try to convince your father and his father. I'm afraid it won't be easy. These men think with their purses and not their hearts."

Her mother's concern was legitimate. Her father and Chin-ho's father should have flatly rejected an arranged marriage between the young couple. Neither family had much to add to the prosperity of the other. They lived side by side in identical houses. Neither family boasted the kind of admirable lineage, advanced education, or special skill that usually made such arrangements viable. But something curious had been happening in the months since Chung-ae and Chin-ho sat together beneath the Chusuk lanterns. Everyone in both of their families, including their fathers, had noticed the strong bond of love developing between the pair.

As it was, when Chung-ae's mother presented her husband with the idea of an arranged marriage between their daughter and the neighbor's son, the fisherman, the old man consented without hesitation. They quickly contacted a Jawoldo matchmaker to broker a deal with Chin-ho's family, who gave the marriage their blessing without reservation. For the first time that anyone could remember on Jawoldo, a couple was going to be married for love.

The wedding day was a celebration for most of Jawoldo's two hundred or so residents. Chin-ho's fishermen friends carried him noisily through streets festooned with wedding lanterns and bright paper streamers. When they arrived at Chung-ae's family house, the end of their circuitous route, the rowdy young men were silenced by what they saw, Chin-ho most of all. There was Chung-ae, dressed in her cardinal-colored wedding hanbok, her long ebony hair drawn back tightly and capped with a crown of flowers. She was the most beautiful young woman on the island that day.

When the ceremony was over, Chin-ho spent three days in her parents' home, as was the custom. Then the newly-weds made the short walk with all of her possessions to a room attached to his father's house. Chung-ae was now a fisherman's wife and she was home.

As poor as they were, their young lives were full of bliss. They fell into the routine that should have lasted them well into their old age. She kept their tiny home, making hot, sour kimchi and sweet, sticky rice cakes, and keeping the charcoal fire that warmed their house burn-ing. He kept venturing out to catch fish and blue crabs to sell in the Incheon market. He'd left his father's boat and was on his own now, spending long, lonely hours on the water, always anxious to return. Their life was simple, and their love was as deep as the Yellow Sea that gave life to everything they knew.

Early one evening, in the spring after their marriage, Chung-ae stood at her door and waited for Chin-ho to bound up the narrow street and sweep her into his arms. She'd wrinkle her nose at the smell of raw fish and crab on his clothes and giggle as he chased her into the kitchen insisting on "key chocko popo," one small kiss. The sun sank into the ocean;

still he didn't come. She waited by the door until it was pitch dark. There was no sound but the wind in the acacia trees. Chin-ho never came home.

Chung-ae spent a fitful night alone, frightened, worried. At daybreak, just as she had done years ago as a young girl, she ran to Jonggol Beach to wait for him. From dawn into early morning she scanned the horizon for his sail, but all she saw were the noisy seabirds and the endless crashing waves. It was a part of the life of a fisherman's wife she'd never imagined. She began to trudge slowly, sadly through sand and up the beach. She saw something. Just a dark shape lying on the side just above the high water mark not far from where Chin-ho normally launched his boat. She felt a sickening lump like a hot stone in her stomach as she quickened her steps to see what it was. She knew in her heart already.

She stood over the dark shape on the beach. Though he was facedown, she knew from his clothing, from the cut of his hair, from his delicate ears. There, a few feet above the thrashing waves, lay her dead husband, Chin-ho. He'd been drowned sometime in the night. She turned him over and saw his body had already been savaged by hermit crabs. She fell to her knees and wept bitter tears over him, her wailing swallowed up by the wind and the crashing surf.

By now, her mother and sister had noticed her missing and had run to the waterfront to find her. They were still well down the beach when they heard her cries. They could see the girl kneeling in the sand, her head in her hands.

"Chung-ae!" the mother shouted. "Chung-ae, what's happened?"

Chung-ae couldn't hear her. As the mother and sister watched in disbelief, the young fisherman's wife stopped crying, stood up, and silently, stoically stepped over the dark shape on the beach at her feet and walked directly into the churning surf.

"Chung-ae! Wait!" the mother shouted, trying her best to run in the soft sand. To no avail. In her grief, Chung-ae could do nothing else but drown herself in a desperate attempt to join her husband in death. Unlike her husband, Chung-ae was swept seaward with the current. Her body was never found. A funeral was held for the young couple in the home of Chin-ho's family. The same two hundred people who had celebrated their marriage with such joy just a few months before were now consumed with the collective grief that strikes a waterfront community whenever the life-giving sea steals back one of their sons or daughters. The people of Jawoldo marched the same dusty lanes, visited the same houses, this time dressed in drab, hand-woven mourning clothes with rough hemp belts.

"It didn't work," Chung-ae's sister told her mother a short time after the funeral.

"What are you talking about?" the mother asked. "What didn't work?"

"Chung-ae could not go to Chin-ho by drowning herself. I saw her."

With great tenderness, the mother pulled Chung-ae's sister close, stroking her hair. "You've been through too much these past few days. But this is nonsense. You know that. Your sister is dead. You couldn't have seen her. None of us will ever see her again."

"But I did see her," the sister protested. "And she's still looking for Chin-ho."

The mother was stunned into silence long enough for the girl to tell her story.

"I was so sad yesterday, Umma. I couldn't bear to sit waiting for the funeral to start. I got up early and went out to the beach. It was still dark and I was standing right where you and I stood when we last saw my sister. And then I heard her. Crying. I ran toward the sound and that's when I saw her all alone, wandering up the beach. She was looking for something. I called to her, but she couldn't hear. When I finally got close, she disappeared like water being poured right into the dry sand.

"She's still looking for him, Umma."

Chung-ae's mother was convinced the visions were caused by the crushing sadness at the loss of her sister, nothing more. Still, there was something about the girl's story that haunted the old woman. Days later, with the funeral now behind them, the mother rose early and went to Janggol Beach. The wind was calm, barely moving the acacia trees that ringed the beach. The sea lapped gently at the sand. Then, a faraway sound, like a screeching tern, too distant to discern clearly. The mother stopped walking and listened in the dark. The sound grew in strange echoing waves and when she finally recognized it, it chilled her to the bone. It was her daughter Chung-ae, crying in anguish.

"Chung-ae! Chung-ae, where are you?"

There was nothing but the growing sound of weeping. In the faint morning light, the old woman could now see the shape of a young woman, kneeling on the beach. The mother approached.

"Chung-ae, it's me."

The ghost looked up, her face a pale, bloated death mask. Kelp and sea grass were stuck in her matted hair. Only her eyes looked alive; they were red and swollen from crying. The old woman was frightened speechless. She stared into the dead face of her daughter until, just as the sister had said, the specter dissolved into the sand leaving nothing but a dark, wet stain on the beach.

In the years since, dozens have witnessed the ghost of the fisherman's wife on the beach of Jawoldo, the island of the red moon. In the predawn hours, Chung-ae can be heard crying on Janggol Beach and those who dare to walk along the waterline are likely to encounter the grieving young widow much as she was in the moments before she took her own life. Strange icy winds whip up sand devils—little tornado-like bursts of fury—that sweep along the beach even when the winds are calm and the ocean is flat. There is one section of the beach where fishermen to this day refuse to pull their boats ashore, fully believing that the sand there is cursed. Keeping a boat there almost surely means catching no fish, they believe, and that's just if you're lucky. Much more dire consequences have been visited on those who ignored the legend of the fisherman's wife, including losing their boats and in some cases their lives to the unforgiving Yellow Sea.

Sarah Tolpin was working as an English teacher in Seoul, South Korea, in 2004 when she decided to take advantage of a rare summer weekend off by hopping a ferry from Incheon to Jawoldo and staying overnight in the old fishing village. A native of Kansas, Sarah was fascinated by the quaint seaside towns with the rows of brightly colored boats. In fact, she couldn't get enough of the ocean. She spent her first day, until well after dark, walking on the beach, collecting shells and small, smooth stones. Reluctantly, she went back to her boardinghouse, anxious to return the next day. On the way back to her room, she noticed an odd monument near the entrance to Janggol Beach. It was a plain, gray cement pillar with the image of a young woman carved in relief on one side. The woman was kneeling amid sand dunes, her hands in front of her face. *She might be praying,* Sarah thought, *or crying.*

Early the next morning, Sarah saw the mysterious monument again as she made her way back to the beach for a predawn stroll. She was only a few steps past the cement pillar when she heard a woman's voice from somewhere down the dark beach. It was the unmistakable sound of crying. Worrying that someone might be hurt or in need of help, Sarah hurried toward the sound. That's when she came upon a real-life version of the scene carved into the pillar. A woman on her knees, hands covering her face, sobbing uncontrollably.

"Are you okay?" Sarah asked, first in English, then in Korean. "Gwan chan ah-yo?"

The ghostly girl looked up at Sarah. A wave of cloying, foul, salty air wafted over the young American teacher. The face of this weeping young woman was pale and bluish in the dim light. Her hands were swollen, blackened, and raw. Seaweed hung all over her like a living death shroud. Sarah screamed. When she did, Chung-ae's ghost melted into the golden sand.

Shaken, Sarah ran back to her room, where she stayed until the ferry was due to leave. Back on board the boat to Incheon, Sarah mustered the nerve to tell a fellow passenger what she'd seen.

"It's just the fisherman's wife," the man told Sarah. "Her story is almost as old as Jawoldo itself."

"Is that the woman on the cement statue near the beach?" Sarah asked.

"That's her," the man said. "Whenever the seas are high, the people of Jawoldo see her, heartbroken and weeping, in the sand. What else could they do but build a monument to her? It's testimony to the deepest love most anyone on that island has ever heard of."

Chapter 12
A Rose-Scented
Dancer

A Kentucky nightclub is an unlikely setting for lovelorn ghosts. But when the place is a former slaughterhouse turned honky-tonk with a murderous past, the spirits of lost sweethearts and jilted lovers just won't leave after last call.

The poison hadn't worked. Her father was sicker, and angrier, but far from dead. Like every other plan she'd had since coming to this awful place, this one was rapidly spinning out of control. Now she found herself walking down to the dingy basement of the old barroom, and she was fairly sure she would never be coming back up. She would end up just like Pearl.

Johanna had never seen the ghost of Pearl Bryan, but she'd heard from enough people in the Latin Quarter nightclub and casino who had seen her spirit to know the sorry story by heart. She was thinking about poor old headless Pearl as she neared the grimy pit at the far corner of the dirt-floored basement. "I wonder if she was scared," Johanna thought, her own heart racing at the thought of what she was about to do. *Surely, she never could have been this desperate,* Johanna thought.

And indeed Johanna had become quite desperate.

Johanna's father, a small-time gangster from Ohio, bought the Latin Quarter in 1953 and ran it with an iron fist. She danced in the club part-time mostly to stave off the boredom that permeated tiny Wilder, Kentucky. That was, until she was swept off her feet by one of the club's new singers, a dashing young man named Robert Randall. The young man lavished attention on her, sending bouquet after bouquet of roses until Johanna's dressing room was filled with the beautiful red flowers and the entire club smelled of their perfume.

She told her father she was in love. Her father said no. Roses or no, there was no way his daughter was going to take up with a lounge singer.

So he was predictably enraged a few months later when Johanna told him that she was pregnant with Robert's child. She thought for sure being pregnant would soften her father's heart on the matter. She was very wrong. Her father contacted his criminal associates and less than twenty-four hours after Johanna's announcement, Robert Randall was found out by Wilder's railroad tracks with two bullets to the back of his head.

"How could he?" she fumed. How could he have the man she loved killed? The father of his own grandchild. Five months into her pregnancy, she decided to try to seek revenge, but she failed miserably. So now, here she was in the Latin Quarter's basement, a pregnant, lovesick bar-owner's daughter about to make one final desperate attempt to join her murdered lover.

Johanna took the vial of poison from her pocket. Half the bottle hadn't been enough to kill her father, probably because of his size and mean disposition, she thought. She hoped the remaining half would work more decisively on her. She gulped down the contents and choked back a wave of nausea as her stomach rebelled against the foul liquid. Already feeling faint, she laid down alongside the filthy hole in the basement floor.

"I'm coming, Robert, my love," she whispered. And in a few minutes she was dead.

It was a far more peaceful ending than Pearl Bryan could have ever hoped for. In fact, the only part of Pearl that had ever seen the inside of the raunchy roadhouse where Johanna lay dead was her neatly shaven, cleanly severed head. Sixty years before Johanna had ever heard of Wilder, Kentucky, Pearl was enduring unspeakable horror at the hands of a man who once said he loved her. Johanna may also have been a victim of love gone wrong, but that's where the similarities ended. That and the fact that two women would end up forever haunting the old honky-tonk now known as Bobby Mackey's Music World.

Pearl Bryan was the charming and attractive daughter of a wealthy farmer in Greencastle, Indiana. Folks around rural Greencastle knew that the outgoing blonde was popular with the boys and had a fair share of suitors. What they could not have guessed is that by late 1895, Pearl was most decidedly, scandalously pregnant.

Pearl had recently started dating a boy named Scott Jackson, a student at the Ohio College of Dental Surgery in Cincinnati. She'd been introduced to Scott by her cousin and trusted friend William Wood, who, like the rest of the Bryan family, saw the handsome young dental student as a fitting match for someone of Pearl's beauty and breeding. When Pearl finally confessed her condition to William in January 1896, the two thought there'd be some explaining to do in terms of timing, but there was no question that Scott Jackson would marry the fair young Bryan girl and make an honest woman of her.

Scott had very different plans, however. He was leading a secret life, delving deep into the black arts, and had
recently taken to performing horrific satanic rituals in a
dilapidated former slaughterhouse in Wilder. The place was
most convenient for such morbid rituals, since it had a huge
open pit in the floor that drained through the groundwater
out into the Licking River. Once used to dispose of blood and
refuse from the slaughterhouse, the bloody well was now a
central prop in the devil-worshiping games Scott and his
associates played.

William Wood broke the news to Scott about Pearl's
pregnancy. Scott asked his friend to send Pearl along to
Cincinnati so they could talk. Both William and Pearl were
convinced this was Scott's prelude to a marriage proposal. It
was actually a death summons.

Pearl Bryan rode the New York Central train from Greencastle to Cincinnati on the morning of January 31, 1896,
arriving at the Third and Central station. Scott met her at the
train, accompanied by a friend and fellow devil-worshiper,
Alonzo Walling. Pearl quickly discovered how wrong she'd
been about Scott's intentions. A loud, public argument
ensued on a Cincinnati street corner as Scott tried to convince Pearl to have an abortion. She refused and threatened
to take the train back to Greencastle immediately.

But Scott Jackson was nothing if not charming. He talked
Pearl into remaining in Ohio so they could discuss their pre-
dicament. Sometime late in the evening on February 1, after
slipping something into the sarsaparilla she was drinking in
a local tavern, Scott convinced Pearl that an abortion was
the answer. Unfortunately for Pearl, Scott was not even a
particularly good dental student, and he certainly was no
doctor. His efforts to help abort the child he'd conceived with

the Indiana farmer's daughter were doomed from the start. He tried giving her cocaine, thinking it would induce labor, but it only made the poor girl more anxious and frightened. At the height of desperation, Scott and Alonzo took Pearl back to Scott's room and tried to perform the abortion using dental instruments. Their inept butchery left Pearl gravely injured and bleeding. Near midnight, fearing they'd already gone too far, Alonzo hired a carriage and he, Scott, and a moaning, crying Pearl Bryan traveled across the Ohio River into Kentucky. There, in a secluded spot near Fort Thomas, the two men murdered Pearl. They cut off her head, which they carried with them in one of Pearl's own travel bags. Her hair was later found in a box in Scott Jackson's apartment.

The next day, the headless body was discovered by passers-by about two hundred feet from Alexandria Turnpike and less than two miles from the abandoned slaughterhouse the men favored for their twisted rituals. The arrest, trial, and execution by hanging of Scott Jackson and Alonzo Walling for Pearl's murder was a sensation, with neither man ever admitting guilt. The gory details exposed during the trial revealed that the missing head of Pearl Bryan had been taken to the old slaughterhouse and used in a satanic ceremony before being dumped down the old blood pit.

The old slaughterhouse was finally boarded up to keep the curious and the ritual seekers out. Newspaper accounts of the time say an "evil eye" fell on many of the people connected to the Pearl Bryan murder case, with several of the detectives and lawyers involved meeting with bad luck and tragedy.

That should have been enough misery and horror for any one small-town building, but the people of Wilder would not let the old slaughterhouse go quietly, despite its sinister past. It was partially torn down in the 1920s, only to be rebuilt as a speakeasy and gambling joint. Murder after bloody murder rocked the rowdy place.

In 1933, E.A. "Buck" Brady bought the building and turned it into the Primrose Club, a bar and casino that was so successful, it quickly caught the attention of organized-crime figures in Cincinnati. They sent small-time hood Albert "Red" Masterson to muscle in on Brady's business and get a piece of the action. Brady responded by shooting Masterson in the leg. Charged with attempted murder, Brady gave up. He sold out to the mob. His club gone, he swore publicly that he would haunt the place to make sure it never thrived as a casino again. Then he shot himself dead in the Primrose's parking lot.

Several owners came and went in the ensuing years. The names and faces changed, but one constant at the old Wilder building was the sense of dark doom that hung over the place. Patrons and employees of the various businesses were reporting strange visions of a headless woman fighting with two men. Bad luck seemed to visit anyone who spent enough time around the place. And woe to those who had reason to be near the musty old pit in the basement. The dark hole seemed to exude evil.

It was into that environment that Johanna's father walked when he bought the place. To the grizzled, ill-tempered old man, the stories were hogwash, superstition, the result of too much booze and too little work. He angrily discouraged any talk of ghosts or haunting in his club. So he never saw the parallel between Pearl, who was five months pregnant when she died, and his own daughter, who had just entered her fifth month when she confessed her condition to him.

In the spring of 1978, country recording artist Bobby Mackey and his wife, Janet, were looking for a place they could turn into a country and western bar. Bobby had his heart set on Nashville, but a chance trip through Wilder changed the Mackeys' lives forever. Bobby fell in love with the tired-looking old roadhouse, he says. To this day, the couple continue to put their hearts and souls into maintaining Bobby Mackey's Music World. The spooky old place often doesn't respond with gratitude to their loving attention.

Ever since he bought the place, Bobby has been contending with supernatural occurrences. The jukebox tends to come on without warning, blaring old tunes from the 1930s and 1940s—songs not loaded into the machine. Chairs whip around without explanation, rooms go ice cold, and employees hear their names called, only to turn and find the club empty.

It was Janet Mackey who first recognized the ghost of Johanna from the overwhelming scent of roses that lingered with the spirit of the forlorn singer. She was in the basement when it first happened. The flowery smell swirled around her and she felt something grab her around the waist.

"It picked me up and threw me back down," the frightened woman told her husband. "I got away from it, and when I got to the top of the stairs there was pressure behind me, pushing me down the steps. I looked back up and a voice was screaming 'Get out! Get out!'"

As she recovered from the fright, another thought stopped her cold. Janet was, just like Johanna and Pearl Bryan before her, five months pregnant at the time.

Carl Lawson was the first employee hired by Bobby when he bought the club. Carl was a loner, mostly content to work as a caretaker and handyman at the tavern in exchange for a meager room upstairs above the bar. It wasn't long before Carl reported seeing and hearing bizarre things in the old building after hours.

He'd double-check the locks and make sure everything was turned off at the end of each night before he went to bed. In the middle of the night, he'd be awakened by the Anniversary Waltz blaring from an unplugged jukebox. When he ran downstairs, he'd find the bar lights on and the doors open. Not long after, Carl ran into Johanna for the first time. When he told Bobby and Janet about the conversations he was having with the mysterious woman in the bar after hours, the owners began to worry about their handyman's sanity.

"And when we're done and she goes away, there's the sweetest scent of roses in the room," Carl added.

It was all Janet needed to hear to be convinced.

Bobby remained skeptical. "I have every penny I own in this place," he told Janet. "I need to make this work. I don't need any ghost stories keeping people away. I need good, positive stuff."

But in 1991, after Carl tried to quell the spirits coming up from the hole in the basement he'd taken to calling Hell's Gate, the supernatural happenings at the club became more frequent and more aggressive. Bobby agreed to try more aggressive measures.

On August 8, 1991, Reverend Glenn Coe performed an exorcism of Carl Lawson and the entire building. The preacher deemed the exorcism a success, but Bobby was so disturbed by what he saw on a videotape of the ritual, he made plans to tear down the building and construct a new club on adjacent property. As he was discussing the plan to demolish the club, a piece of the ceiling fell on him. Undaunted, he went ahead with the plans, until it was discovered that a huge, sixty-foot deep fissure ran from the well in the basement of the old slaughterhouse straight through Bobby's new property next door. The new lot was useless for building.

So Bobby Mackey's Music World remains in the old slaughterhouse with the restless ghosts of Pearl and Johanna and countless others. Mackey made peace with the spiritual interlopers by penning a ballad called "Johanna," which he performs nightly. It seems, for now, to have appeased at least some of the ghosts in his nightclub.

Still, Bobby has installed a sign near the front door of his club by way of fair warning.

"Warning to our patrons," the sign reads. "This establishment is purported to be haunted. The management is not responsible and cannot be held liable for any actions of any ghosts/spirits on this premises."

Chapter 13

Angry Widow of Marrero's Mansion

He lured her away from her home and family with a mansion in a tropical paradise. But when Francisco Marrero's polygamous past came back to haunt her, she vowed to remain forever in the house that love built.

"Because you are beautiful," Francisco told her. "And I love you. Isn't that enough?"

Enriquetta smiled shyly. Francisco Marrero was much older than she. He wore expensive suits and traveled the world. He was the richest man she'd ever known. And for the past three months he'd been pursuing her, buying her gifts, bringing her jewelry.

She'd never traveled very far outside of her small Cuban village near Gibara. Now he was asking her to go to America, to be his wife in another country. It seemed impossible to her. Completely unreal.

"What about my mother and father?" she asked. "Who will care for them?'

"I will see that they are well taken care of, Enriquetta," Francisco told her. "With you as my wife, your family will want for nothing."

"Where would we live?" she asked.

Francisco smiled at the question. He'd been waiting for her to ask.

"Come, my dear. Come with me."

They went to a small wrought-iron table on the porch. Francisco pulled out several neatly folded papers from his jacket pocket. He spread them out on the table. They were architectural drawings, faint blue lines on sepia-toned paper. Enriquetta could make out the image of a grand, ornate house far bigger than anything she'd ever seen, or even imagined.

It was a tropical mansion. Great columns separated two glorious porches, one above the other. Every one of the magnificent windows was trimmed with finely detailed molding and sturdy-looking shutters.

"What is this place?" Enriquetta asked innocently.

"This is my new bride's American home," Francisco said.

The house, at least the drawing of it, was magnificent. But in her heart, Enriquetta knew Francisco was also sincere about his feelings for her. She could sense it. He'd had this house designed to lure her to America. But it was the sweet way he wooed her, worked to gain her trust, pleaded for her hand, that finally won her over.

She'd been told since she was a child that she was beautiful, too beautiful for her rustic little fishing village. But she'd never really felt it. She'd never wanted to marry a rich man just for the sake of leaving the home of her parents. What she wanted more than anything was to love and be loved. She wanted to live the way her mother and father lived. She watched how sweetly her parents still looked at each other. It wouldn't matter where on earth she ended up if she could simply grow old in the company of someone who loved her just that much.

And that was how Francisco was looking at her now. He would, she believed, look at her that way forever. That's when she first realized that she loved him.

And so she agreed. With Francisco's resources it took

little time to make the arrangements. By 1889, he'd become one of the richest cigar exporters in the world. The new mansion he'd built for his young wife in the heart of Key West, Florida, would make a formidable base of operations for his business as well. There seemed to be very little that could upset the couple's pursuit of happiness as the priest in Cuba pronounced them man and wife. They set off for America the following morning.

"Oh, Francisco, it's so beautiful," Enriquetta said as he led her from the carriage to the steps of their new Fleming Street home. It was just two blocks from the warm waters of the Gulf of Mexico. The same balmy ocean surrounded her home in Gibara, and yet, this place seemed like another world entirely. She started to cry.

"Come, my dear. Don't cry. As long as I'm alive, there's nothing but happiness for you here."

And Francisco Marrero kept to the letter of his promise. The couple made a wonderful, warm home of their mansion on Fleming Street. He traveled between Florida, Cuba, and Europe building his cigar business and amassing even greater wealth. Enriquetta was always the faithful, adoring wife, waiting eagerly for her husband's return. Within a decade, all of those passionate homecomings had brought Francisco and Enriquetta Marrero eight beautiful children.

"When will you be back, my love?" Enriquetta asked one fall morning. It was early 1901. Francisco was packing a small travel bag for another routine trip to Havana.

"I'll be gone just one night," he said. "I'll be back on the late afternoon boat tomorrow, as usual."

There was something about his voice that worried her, some tension that was foreign to her.

"Is everything all right, Francisco?"

"Just routine business," he said absently. Then he turned to her and kissed her cheek. "Nothing for my beautiful wife to be concerned about."

"Maybe it's time for you to travel less," Enriquetta said.

"Hush, woman," he joked with her. "Take care of the kids and yourself, my dear. I love you. I'll be back soon."

Francisco left as he always did, on the early boat that sailed from the dock at the foot of Duvall Street. Enriquetta spent the rest of the afternoon with a discomfort she could not explain. She told herself she was being silly. She busied herself taking care of the children and preparing for a lonely night at home.

The next morning, her anxiety hadn't eased. She went for a walk along the docks to clear her head. She looked out across the Gulf and wondered what Gibara looked like today. She wondered what Francisco was doing at that moment, if he was looking out at the ocean too, if he was thinking of her.

That's when a fear like she'd never known swept over her. Something was wrong, she knew it.

When the afternoon ferry arrived, Francisco was not on it. She began to ask his business associates around Key West, but none of them had heard anything. She went back home and sat on the wide front porch, rocking absently in the wicker rocker and staring down toward the sea.

"Mrs. Marrero? Enriquetta Marrero?"

Enriquetta jumped. The young man had startled her. He was wearing a dark, drab suit with a black tie. He was showing her a badge pinned into his wallet.

"My name is Eduardo Santos," the young man said. "I'm a U.S. Customs inspector. May I speak with you?"

"Of course. Please sit down."

"That's okay, ma'am. I'll stand. Are you the wife of Francisco Marrero?"

"Yes. Yes, I am. Is something wrong?"

"I'm afraid I have bad news, ma'am." He corrected himself. "Terrible news."

"Oh my God, what is it? Is Francisco all right? Is he in trouble?"

The young man didn't know where to began, so he sat down slowly on the edge of one of the porch rockers and rubbed his temple. Best to start with the worst, he figured.

"He's dead, Mrs. Marrero. I'm very sorry. The U.S. Customs Department wishes to express its—"

"What in the world are you saying?" Enriquetta interrupted. "My husband cannot be dead. He went to Cuba to order cigars. He's coming home. We have eight children. He can't be."

Overcome, she started to cry.

Agent Santos did his best to comfort her. He felt he owed her some explanation, so he did his best to tell her the story, though she didn't appear to be really listening or understanding his words.

Francisco had gone to Cuba this time to do business and to help Customs agents gather information on other cigar traders who were avoiding tariffs by shipping goods through fake holding companies scattered around the Caribbean. In fact, Francisco had been helping the U.S. government for several years, giving them information on his dishonest competitors. On this trip, however, something had gone wrong. The man Francisco thought was an agent of the government was actually working for the smugglers. When they discovered Francisco was an informant, they killed him. He was found stabbed to death in a Havana alley.

The next few days were a blur for Enriquetta. There were funeral arrangements to make, affairs to settle, finances to figure out. And how would she explain to eight children that their father was never again coming home? The first thing she had to do was arrange for her husband's body to be brought from Cuba. She contacted authorities who assured her his remains would be on the afternoon boat the following morning.

"Have the casket brought directly to our home," Enriquetta requested. "We'll have the funeral here, in the place we both loved so much."

But the following day, well after the afternoon boat should have arrived, there was no sign of the couriers or her husband's body. She waited anxiously on the porch. That's when she saw them coming, marching up Fleming Street with purpose. A heavy-set woman with a wild mane of jet-black hair was followed by two younger men in business suits. One of the men had a leather bag of the type lawyers generally carried. When they were about a block away, it was clear they were heading for her house.

Enriquetta tried to greet them on the steps, but the woman pushed her way past and bounded up onto the porch. The two men followed.

"I'm sorry, can I help you?" Enriquetta asked.

"Is this the house of Francisco Marrero?" the big woman asked, looking up and down the grand facade of the mansion.

"Yes it is, may I ask—"

"Then this is my house," the woman shot back. "You'll have to leave."

"Who are you?" Enriquetta asked, stunned.

"I am Maria Garcia Marrero. I am Francisco's widow."

The woman glared at Enriquetta.

"But how . . . ?"

"Explain it to her, then get her out of here," the woman told the young man with the leather bag.

The lawyer did his best to be gentle as he showed Enriquetta the documents. Indeed, Maria was Francisco's wife from Havana. They'd been married for seven years before he left her and married Enriquetta. But there had never been a divorce. So the marriage to Maria was valid. The marriage to Enriquetta was not. Maria Garcia Marrero was the rightful owner of all of Francisco's assets. Including the house he'd built to win Enriquetta's love.

"But where will I go? What about my children?"

"I'm sorry, ma'am. Neither you nor they have any claim to the Marrero estate."

"And what about my husband's body?"

Maria jumped up to answer. "My husband had a proper funeral in Cuba. He's been buried already."

The police eventually showed up to help the young lawyers execute the orders they carried. As Enriquetta was escorted from the house for the last time, she stopped and turned to Maria, her rage finally boiling over.

"Neither you nor anyone else will ever find peace in this house. Curse you and everyone that comes after you," Enriquetta spat. "With God as my witness, I will always remain here in spirit."

With that, she was gone. She sailed back to the tiny village near Gibara. They tried to live, she and her eight children, in the two-room shack she'd once shared with her parents. But the strain was too great, the heartbreak too immense, the unfairness too overwhelming. Within a few months, Enriquetta became very sick. One by one, the children succumbed to tuberculosis or diphtheria, both of which were sweeping the island. With little will to continue, her broken heart simply gave out. She died with loving words for Francisco on her lips.

It is the words that she spoke to Maria, however, that continue to reverberate though the plush halls of Marrero's Guest Mansion, one of Key West's most quaint and comfortable lodging houses. Almost since the day she died, the place has been the scene of mysterious happenings, ghostly visions, and, especially, the sound of crying children in the home's former nurseries, now guest rooms numbered 17 and 23. Guests often smell Enriquetta's lavender perfume wafting through the halls, and more than a few have woken up to find the ghostly woman sitting on the edge of their beds, or standing before one of the room's full-length mirrors, brushing her long, dark hair.

In room 18, the room Enriquetta and Francisco used as their own bedroom, a ghostly apparition of Enriquetta is often seen passing like vapor through the walls and closed doors. It was in that room that Peter Fitzgerald came face to ghostly face with the eternally bitter Enriquetta.

Peter and his wife, Samantha, traveled from frigid Rhode Island to balmy Key West in the winter of 2003, intent on finding a sunny spot to spend an impromptu second honeymoon. While researching places to stay in Key West, Peter came across a brief account of Enriquetta's tragic story and the ghost legends it spawned, but didn't think much of it. He decided not to tell his wife, however, worried that the woeful tale might put a damper on their romantic getaway.

As they settled into room 18 at the Marrero Mansion, Samantha surprised him with a question.

"Do you know about the ghost of the angry widow here?" she asked.

"What in the world are you talking about?"

"I was in the lobby and I heard some people talking about a widow who lost this home when her husband died. They say her ghost still haunts the place."

"That's ridiculous," Peter protested. "There's no angry widow ghost. There's no ghosts, period."

As if punctuating the last word of his denial, there was a sharp click at the door. Samantha ran and tried the handle. It was locked. From the outside. They were trapped in their room. The lights began to flash on and off and the sound of children crying could be clearly heard coming from the next room. Peter felt a chill and turned, expecting to find an open window, but found himself staring at a blank wall. The pattern on the wallpaper held his gaze. It seemed to be moving, changing, almost breathing, he thought to himself. And suddenly he was face-to-face with her. The ghostly woman materialized from the swimming pattern on the wall and the crazy shadows being cast by the flashing room lights. The specter was just inches from him. He held his breath.

As Peter and Samantha watched, horrified, the ghost of Enriquetta Marrero drifted across their room—across her room—and vanished through the wall heading toward the sound of the crying children. After she passed, the crying stopped, the lights stopped flickering, and the door unlocked and popped open, with a loud snap.

The couple made excuses about a family emergency back home and checked out immediately. This was not, Peter told his wife, the kind of place he hoped to relax and celebrate their love. Clearly, Enriquetta has other ideas. For a woman who was cheated out of love and life, the Key West mansion is exactly where she intends to remain.

Chapter 14
Soldier in the Barrel

On the wind-swept shore of Lake Ontario a soldier on the run from the enemy couldn't resist one last rendezvous with his beautiful girlfriend. Following his heart led to his death and left him a permanent—and much heralded—guest in a historic Canadian inn.

Brian had been looking forward to this trip to Niagara-on-the-Lake for months. It was a chance for him and Paula to get away for a few days, enjoy the Shaw Festival theaters, tour the local wineries, and maybe get down to see the falls. He knew Paula had been looking forward to it as well. She was the main reason he was keeping his anger in check and swallowing his instinct to turn around and head back home.

She could tell something was bothering him.

"It's a beautiful old inn, don't you think?" Paula asked, trying to gauge what was wrong.

"Sure, seems fine," Brian said, taking in the bright, lemon-colored clapboard and the coal-black shutters of the stately Olde Angel Inn. And it was fine, except for one thing.

Brian, a government auditor in Montreal, was as proud a Canadian as there was. As such, he was perplexed by the most striking feature of the Olde Angel Inn from where he stood. Above the front door of the place, where any self-respecting Canadian would expect to see the bold, red maple leaf of Canada's flag, there was instead a British Union Jack whipping proudly in the Niagara breeze.

"It's the flag, isn't it?" Paula asked, finally catching on.

"It just seems odd, is all," he said. "Do we want to stay in a place that's so . . . British?"

"Yes," Paula said, playfully pulling his hand and dragging him toward the entrance. "Yes, we do."

When the couple got to the front desk, they found the clerk exceptionally polite. Polite enough, Brian thought, to ask about the uncomfortable matter of the flag flying above the old inn.

"Are you a Canadian, then?" Brian asked.

"Brian!" Paula interrupted. "Stop!"

"That's okay, ma'am," the clerk replied matter-of-factly. "I am a Canadian. I've lived in Ontario all of my life. And my parents and their parents as well. Why do you ask?"

"It's about your flag," Brian continued. "I couldn't help but notice that . . ."

"That it's British?"

"Yes, right. British. Exactly."

"There's a very good reason for that. Once you've stayed with us, you'll sincerely hope never to see any other colors flying over our doorway."

"And why is that?" asked Brian.

"Because that's what keeps him from wandering throughout the inn."

Before Brian or Paula could say anything, the clerk slid from behind the counter and gestured for them to follow. When they reached the entryway near the front door, the clerk pointed to a metal plaque on the wall, engraved with narrow block letters.

The couple read the inscription.

"Local folklore has it that this inn is haunted by the ghost of a British soldier killed at the old inn during the

War of 1812. He is said to walk the inn's cellars after dark, never visiting the upper floors so long as a Union Jack flies above the inn's door."

Brian and Paula were speechless.

"There's a ghost?" Paula finally asked.

As he'd done with countless other guests before them, the clerk brought the couple to the cozy lounge known as The Snug and told them the story of Colin Swayze, the inn's only permanent guest and a man who let love cloud his judgment in a fatal way. And it began nearly two centuries ago, when the war-torn area all around the Olde Angel Inn was known as Newark.

The streets were already thick with smoke, and the steady pounding of the American cannons was growing in intensity. The War of 1812 was less than a year old, but already the Yanks had the British in Ontario on the run. There'd been a rout in Niagara and now the Americans were taking Newark. The Canadian conscripts who had signed on to fight for the British were fleeing in desperate retreat. All except Captain Colin Swayze. He was standing, alone, on King Street watching the black smoke billow from a town twenty miles to the south. The Americans were burning the villages flat as they approached.

Swayze cut through the market alley toward Regent Street until he came to the inn known as the Harmonious Coach House. He ducked inside, the sound of enemy artillery reverberating off the wooden buildings all around him.

"Colin!" Euretta shouted when she saw him. "I thought you'd left."

Euretta was striking, with her long, dark hair and darker eyes. The ravages of war had turned everything in Newark drab and gray, but the daughter of the coach house's owner continued to grace the inn with her youthful beauty. And the reason for the sparkle in her eyes and her easy smile was the man now reaching to embrace her.

"I couldn't leave without seeing you again," Colin said.

Through the early evening, the young soldier and his beloved innkeeper's daughter held each other and listened as the big American guns rolled closer to the town center. When the reports shattered the coach house's attic windows, Euretta took Colin's face in her hands and brought her lips close to his ear.

"You must leave now," she whispered through tears. "There's still time."

"Never," he replied. "I won't leave you. I'll hide here and when the Americans pass, we'll leave together."

No sooner were the words out than the couple heard the shouts of the American soldiers at the door. Colin grabbed his cloak and his gun and ran down the basement steps into the dark storage cellar. In the pitch black he felt his way around, desperate for a place to hide. He knew the Americans would search every corner of the place. In a far corner of the cellar he stumbled into a pile of beer barrels. Colin pried the lid off of one of the barrels and tossed his cloak and gun inside, then he crawled inside and pulled the lid shut above his head.

"Where are the soldiers?" the American lieutenant shouted at Euretta.

"I'm telling you there's no one here but my father and me," she replied. She glared at the intruders, unafraid. "The soldiers have all fled, and all of our guests have been frightened away. You must have seen them all running north. Why don't you just go and leave us alone?"

The lieutenant turned to his comrades. "Search the place. If she's telling the truth, we'll leave them alone. If she's lying, burn the place to the ground."

With that, a squad of a dozen men began ransacking the coach house, upsetting every cabinet, tearing the contents from every closet. After they'd searched all of the rooms, they rested in The Snug, helping themselves to the liquor behind the inn's bar. After about an hour, they were getting loud and comfortable. Euretta approached the lieutenant.

"So. You've found nothing. Will you go now?"

"You're quite bold, my dear innkeeper's daughter. And quite beautiful too," the soldier slurred. "Why don't you sit and drink with me?"

From the shadows, Euretta's father leapt forward and grabbed the lieutenant's whiskey glass, throwing the drink in the American's face.

"There!" the old man shouted. "You've had your drink with her. Now get out of my inn. Get out!"

The American stood and shoved the old man to the floor, to the delight of the inebriated soldiers in the tiny tavern. As he stood over her father, he saw young Euretta, her pretty young face twisted with anger and sadness. It snapped the lieutenant from his drunken foolishness.

"All right, men. Enough of this. Our search is done here. Let us go, as we promised."

The Americans gathered their things together with what they'd managed to steal from the coach house guest rooms. The entire squad was making its way out the door when there was a shout from back inside the house. One of the younger American soldiers, just a boy really, was calling.

"Lieutenant, sir. A moment please."

"What is it, Corporal?" the officer asked.

"Sir, there's one place we haven't checked. I've found stairs down to a basement, sir."

The rest of the American contingent grumbled impatiently. They were laden with stolen goods and had their fill of beer and whiskey. They wanted to be on their way. They had no desire to go poking around the dank cellar on some fool's errand. The lieutenant, however, remained silent. As the rest of the men shuffled back inside the inn, the officer kept his gaze firmly on Euretta. He'd sensed something when the boy mentioned the basement, he thought. A frown. A flinch, however brief. There was something down there.

"Search it!" the lieutenant ordered loudly.

The squad thundered down the rickety, narrow steps into the cellar. The torches they used to light the way glinted off their bayonets as they stabbed at piles of grain bags and potato crates. Every place that could hide a man was run through with cold steel. By the time they made their way back to the beer barrel storage room, they'd become almost mechanical, fatally efficient. Each barrel was pierced swiftly in three places, leaving no room for doubt or error.

When they were done, the lieutenant held his hand up for silence. There was no sound at all in the cellar, just the quiet crying of the young innkeeper's daughter drifting down on them from the floor above. The soldiers climbed the steps and exited the house. The officer stopped on the way out, turning to Euretta.

"You kept your word. There was no one here. Now we'll keep ours. We'll leave you now."

And they were gone.

As soon as the Americans were out of sight, Euretta ran to the basement. To find her lover.

"Colin?" she called. "Colin, are you here?"

No response. She held a lantern out in front of her as she made her way deeper into the cellar. Finally, she was standing amid the pile of beer barrels, each ruined with holes on all sides. She saw one barrel in the far corner still standing upright, the bayonet slashes barely visible between the staves. She stepped closer and the lantern revealed a pool of blood thickening on the dirt floor around the keg.

"Oh, Colin," she whispered.

She set the lantern down and pried open the barrel top. Inside was the body of her lover, Captain Colin Swayze, stabbed through the heart and lungs by the searchers' bayonets. Though the pain must have been excruciating, he never cried out, likely saving the lives of Euretta and her father and most certainly keeping the coach house from being burned down by the invaders. It quickly became evident that the young Captain Swayze had no intention of leaving the place he'd given his life to spare.

"Amazing," Brian said when the clerk had finished the tale. "So when did folks first see his ghost?"

"It didn't take long at all," the clerk said. "Wait here."

The inn employee got up and went over to the front desk, fishing around beneath the counter. He returned with a few slips of folded, yellowed, tissue-thin paper. He spread them out on the table in front of the couple.

"Less than a decade after he was killed, Captain Swayze was already making news," the clerk said. "Here, look at these newspaper clippings."

The couple leaned forward to read the faded newsprint. The date on the clipping was October 13, 1821.

REPORTS HAVE BEEN received of frequent distur-
bances during the night at the Olde Angel Inn. Local
authorities have declined an investigation, pending
a formal complaint or the discovery of evidence of
wrongdoing.

Upon independent inquiry, this editor has received information of a most unsettling nature
which will raise and terrify the reader's imagination.
The popular explanation provided by hotel guests
and local patrons, attributes the nocturnal distur-
bances to Permutations of the Spirit World. In short,
there is a Ghost haunting the Olde Angel Inn.

Footsteps have been heard coming from the
darkened dining room, although the source of
the sound could not be determined. The clinking
of glasses, laughter and conversation have echoed
throughout the Inn, as if emanating from thin air.
Most disturbing was the discovery by the serving
staff of table settings, set that previous evening,
having been mysteriously arranged.

The Inn's respected proprietor will not dismiss the
reports nor contradict the Existence of Apparitions.

The Reader should be mindful of the many unexplained Forces of Nature. There are also those who
credit the appearance of Ghosts and Specters to a
tragic past occurrence with an unresolved outcome.
Such is the circumstance at the Olde Angel Inn.

Some believe the Ghost of Captain Swayze is
fated to walk the Inn at night, perhaps in longing
for his lost love. Others suggest the Captain stands
sentinel, protecting the property against foreign invaders. It is said that his ghost will remain harmless

as long as the British flag flies over the Inn, a precaution prudently taken by the proprietor.

If any Reader thinks these facts incredible, let him enjoy his opinion, but this writer will follow with interest any reports of ghostly encounters at the Olde Angel Inn.

Other papers in the ancient stack included other details of the hauntings over the past two centuries. The sound of shuffling boots and rattling barrels coming from a dark and empty cellar, weird shouts from vacant rooms, and even sightings of Captain Swayze's ghost patrolling the inn and, perhaps, hoping for one last encounter with the beautiful young woman he loved.

Brian shuffled through the papers and was struck by one particularly detailed encounter. Brian read aloud for Paula and the clerk, though the inn employee knew the story by heart.

It happened on March 17, 1939. A lone traveler identified only as Norris was asleep in a room on the first floor of the inn, directly above the old barrel vault. Well after midnight, a persistent clatter from beneath his floor awoke him. Annoyed at what he assumed were workers making a ruckus in the room below him, Norris grabbed his cane from the bedpost and, without getting out of bed, rapped the stick against the floor angrily. The clatter below stopped. Satisfied, Norris set his cane down and closed his eyes. Suddenly the room turned frigid. Norris pulled the blankets tight around him against the sudden cold. Now there came a low moaning, like the sound of a man in pain. It was coming from the floor beside the bed.

Norris slowly, cautiously turned to look at the floor of his room. What he saw petrified him. A translucent, vaporous shape was appearing through the floorboards. It was the top of a man's head. As Norris continued to watch in horror, the ghost rose up through the floor until the entire specter of a young man in military garb was standing over him, leering down at the frightened guest huddled in his bed.

The ghost was silent. It simply stood over the man, glaring down at him in the ice-cold room. The curtains fluttered wildly though the windows were shut tight. After several long minutes the ghost began to retreat to its cellar lair, drifting back down through the floor in the same way it arrived.

Norris rose from his bed, quickly collected his things, and checked out, preferring to travel onward to Quebec in the dead of night than spend another minute in the haunted Olde Angel Inn.

"So you've heard and read the stories, you know about the flag and about the ghost and about the love story that connects them both," the clerk said. "Now I have to ask you what I ask everyone. Do you still want to stay here?"

Paula smiled and nodded.

"Absolutely we do," Brian said. "What couple can resist a tale of love and devotion like that? Just do us a small favor, would you?"

"Certainly, sir," said the employee. "What is it?"

"Well, I wouldn't want my colleagues back up in Montreal to hear this," Brian answered, "but please, let's leave the British flag flying out front, shall we?"

Chapter 15

The Lady
of the Lake

Long Island's largest lake holds a dark secret of forbidden romance and tragedy. For one desperate young girl, it was the place where she gave up her dream of true love. And nearly every summer since, it's been the place where young men fall victim to her curse.

She expected to be pulled down in the black water for all eternity.

Everyone in her tribe believed the lake to be bottomless and she never thought to question it. At some point, with the weight pulling her deeper and deeper, she would drown, of course. She knew that. But her body, she thought, would continue to sink forever in the icy waters of the lake her Setauket tribe called Ronkonkoma.

Alone, she rowed the canoe toward the center of the lake, guided by a bright, midsummer full moon. Her paddle made the only ripples on the water, save for the occasional rainbow trout breaking the surface to take a struggling mayfly. When she was as far from the opposite shore as she was from her home, she stopped rowing. She could see the fires from the white man's camp. She knew the one they called Hugh was there. Somewhere out there across the onyx surface of the lake, he was waiting for her. By now he was wondering why she hadn't rowed to the camp to see him, as she'd promised. He had no idea that he'd never see her again.

She loosened the sinew and leather cord tied around her waist and set it aside. She removed her deerskin dress and laid it out on the floor of the canoe. For a moment, she sat there quietly in the moonlight, feeling the cool night air on her skin. The haunting sound of a single whippoorwill came from somewhere on the far side of the lake.

All she wanted was someone to hold and to love. She'd found it in the white man they called Hugh. And he loved her. She wanted to leave her tribe and be with him. But the elders had refused to even listen to such a proposal. She was forbidden from marrying even a man from one of the other three native tribes around Ronkonkoma. There was surely no way she would ever be allowed to have a relationship with some white stranger. When she protested, her father, the tribe's sachem, or leader, ordered her confined to the sleeping lodge whenever she wasn't gathering wood or water or picking the ripe blueberries and blackberries that lined the banks of the lake. Hugh was told he would surely be killed if he ever walked on Setauket land again.

The last time she'd seen him was in that summer of 1634. She'd slipped away from a group of women picking berries and run along the shore to the place where the Unke-chaug land began. They'd met there before. She knew he'd be there, and he was. They hid in the thick brush and held each other. When they parted, he said he loved her. She told him that on the next full moon, she would steal away and row across the lake to be with him forever. She raced back to the berry patches, but the women were already gone. When she returned to her camp, her father looked at her with anger and suspicion.

"If you were ever to leave the tribe, I would not rest until this white man they call Hugh was dead," he told her.

"We would go to war with these white men and kill them all or else be killed ourselves, down to every last man."

"I understand," the girl answered quietly, her head bowed.

And so now she sat naked in the tiny canoe, unable to paddle the rest of the way across the lake to join her lover lest she incite a battle in which many would be killed. She began to take the stones she was hauling in the rear of the little boat and placed them on the dress. She folded the deerskin into a bag with the stones inside, fastening the top with a bit of vine. She took the sinew belt and tied her ankles together with one end. The other end she tied to the top of the stone-filled dress. She gathered the weighted bundle into her lap. The whippoorwill called again, filling her with unbearable sadness. Her eyes filled with tears, and she tilted the canoe sharply to one side and rolled out into the inky water. The weights tied to her feet pulled her quickly out of sight.

The following morning, the Setauket camp was abuzz with the news that the girl was missing. Her father was already making plans to gather braves and attack the white man's camp on the far shore of the lake. He was stopped by a group of men who had been out on the lake fishing before dawn. They'd found the overturned canoe adrift in the still water in the middle of Ronkonkoma. As the men were discussing the possible meaning of the upset boat, two women came out of the sleeping lodge crying and screaming. Beside the girl's bed, they found a simple drawing in the dirt; a large circle with waves and a small person in the middle with head pointed down. The meaning was as clear as the Ronkonkoma waters. She was drowned in the lake.

What frightened the women most, however, was what else the girl had drawn. A straight line with arrow-pointed ends cut across the bottom edge of the circle. In simple imagery, she'd cut off the tribe from the life-giving power of the lake. She wanted the place to be cursed to them forever.

The gathering war party quickly turned to mourning. One of the most beautiful young women of the tribe was lost. The father screamed in anguish and the women cried well into the night.

The pitiful wailing sounds could be heard in the white man's camp across the lake. The man they called Hugh, a woodcutter named Hugh Birdsall, heard it and was overcome with grief. When the girl hadn't shown up as promised, he'd feared the worst. And now he knew for sure that she was dead.

All three of the boys knew the centuries-old story of the Indian maiden whose ghost had come to be known as Ronkonkoma's Lady of the Lake. Van Halen's "Eruption" was blaring from the car stereo as they stripped off their shirts in the parking lot of Long Island's Brookhaven Town Beach. It was nearing midnight on an exceptionally warm June night in 1983. The trio were just a week away from graduating from high school and they'd come to the lake on a dare.

"How far are we going, Paul?" one of the boys asked.

"Me and Chuck will swim out to the old diving raft, touch it, and come back," Paul answered. "That should be enough time for her to get us if she's gonna get us."

He laughed out loud at his own morbid assessment, but Chuck and his twin brother, Chad, remained silent.

"Chad, stay here and watch out for the cops and flash the headlights if there's trouble," Paul continued.

"Whose dumb idea was this anyway?" Chad asked.

"We gotta do this," Paul said. "We said we would."

Paul and Chuck waded into the water, which was much colder than the night air.

"Oh man, it's freezing!" Chuck shouted.

"Ssshh . . . quiet, man. Someone's gonna call the cops."

By the time Chuck had managed to get himself chest deep in the chilly lake, Paul was already swimming easily out into the darkness.

"Hey, wait up!" Chuck yelled. He began thrashing his way toward the diving platform. In the faint moonlight, the old float was just barely visible about fifty yards off the beach. Paul reached it first, touching the slick, algae-covered planking, then pulling himself up on his elbows, resting halfway out of the water. He waited for Chuck.

Chuck was not a graceful swimmer, but he seemed to be in no danger as he splashed and paddled toward Paul. Suddenly, Chuck let out a water-choked grunt. He was no longer swimming but was struggling to tread water. The sound caught Paul's attention. He strained to see Chuck in the darkness. He was still thirty feet from the raft.

"What's wrong, man?" Paul shouted into the dark.

"Something touched me!" Chuck yelled back. His voice was high and panicked. He was struggling to keep his head above the water. "It's grabbing me, Paul. Help!"

"Just be cool, keep swimming toward my voice. You're almost there."

"I can't, man. I'm not gonna make it."

Paul pushed himself off the platform and swam toward his friend. When he got there, he tried to grab Chuck's arms, but the boy was panicking. Chuck reached out and grabbed Paul around the neck, threatening to drown them both. Paul slipped out of the grasp and came up behind Chuck, grabbing him around the shoulders and pulling him toward the diving raft.

As the pair moved through the black water, Paul could feel a weight dragging them down—something much heavier than Chuck's body alone. It took all of Paul's strength to haul himself and his friend onto the raft. When they were safely out of the water, Chuck laid his head against the wet, slimy surface of the raft, trying to catch his breath. The boys lay on the raft for a long time saying nothing. Finally, Paul spoke.

"What happened out there?"

"It was her."

"How do you know?"

"What the hell else could it be, Paul?!" Chuck shouted. He took a breath to steady his voice. "I'm sorry, man. But seriously, I felt hands sliding up my legs. And when they got up around my waist, they grabbed me hard and tried to pull me under. She was too strong. I couldn't have fought it alone. If you hadn't been here . . ."

The last part was left to drift into the feeble moonlight sparkling on the mirror surface of the lake.

The boys sat on the raft, too frightened to get back into the water. After about an hour they saw the headlights on Chad's car flash several times, then go out completely. The parking lot of the town beach began to dance with the blue and white flashing lights of a local police cruiser. From out on the diving platform, the boys could hear the voices but couldn't make out what was being said. Thirty minutes later, it became evident. A police van backed a trailer with a small flat-bottomed boat into the lake. In short order, the boys were picked up from the raft and ferried back to shore, where they got a lecture on trespassing on the beach after hours.

The warning was unnecessary. None of the three boys ever went near the waters of Lake Ronkonkoma again. Others, however, have not been so lucky. The ghost of Tuskawanta, or the Lady of the Lake, as she's known to everyone on Long Island, claims at least one young man every summer, according to the legend. Historical society records dating back to 1877 indicate more than 130 drownings in Lake Ronkonkoma. County documents detail forty-five drownings in the lake since 1963, and every one of them was a young man.

Those lucky enough to survive, those like Chuck and Paul, say they felt hands clutching them from beneath the murky water or being pulled into the depths by mysterious whirlpools whipped up in the center of Ronkonkoma. One of the police officers shuttling Chuck and Paul back to the beach that night in the little skiff told them he'd worked for several summers as a lifeguard on the beaches on Lake Ronkonkoma. He told them that the tricky thing about the waters of Ronkonkoma was how deep the placid, harmless-looking body of water really was. It didn't get much deeper than ten feet in most places. But there were spots on the lake, including the area where the boys were just swimming, that dropped off to forty, fifty, even eighty feet deep.

The thing that used to mystify the Native Americans and the early white settlers alike, the officer said, was how, after the death of the young Setauket maiden, the level of the lake seemed to rise and fall of its own accord without regard for the rainfall or the weather.

"So did you ever see her?" the shaken young men asked. "Like when you worked here, did you ever feel her hands or see anyone else get taken under?"

"I'll tell you what. I used to have nightmares all the time about trying to rescue someone," the cop told the boys. "Desperate dreams of swimming and swimming but never being able to save them. Whenever I had those dreams I knew someone was going to die in this lake. And they always did."

"Why does she do it?" Chuck asked absently, still rubbing the sore spot on his hip where he'd felt the hands grabbing him, pulling him.

The cop thought about it.

"This Indian maiden, she may have given up on her one true love. But I guess she's never quit trying to capture some other young man just like him."

Chapter 16
Mitchell's Curse

Few have seen the ghost of Anne Mitchell, but that doesn't mean her spirit hasn't had a profound impact on Mount Sterling, Kentucky. Forced to abandon her true love and marry a man she cared nothing for, Anne laid a fatal curse on her family home that continued to wreak havoc long after she was struck dead.

She was certain she heard it that time. The slightest creak, the snap of a dry twig. Anne stopped in her tracks and tried to peer into the underbrush in the pitch-black forest. It was no use. This hour of night, she could barely see where she was going, much less determine the source of the sound.

"Who's there?" she called in a shouted whisper.

There was no response.

Anne was a rare beauty, and a bold—some said defiant—young woman of the kind that made the Mitchell family one of the most admired and respected in central Kentucky's genteel society. But out here, poking her way slowly along a cow path in the dark woods—her ebony hair pulled back tightly to ward off the briars and low branches—she felt small, frightened. And there was that unnerving noise, as if someone or something was following her.

She took a deep breath. She was on her way to meet her true love, the man of her dreams, she reminded herself. That gave her courage. She started moving forward again and this time she was sure she heard a rustling, closer this time. Anne started to run up the path to a clearing where a logging road crossed through the woods. The moonlight was brighter here, staining everything a steely blue. She ducked behind a stump, waiting to see what emerged from the path into the open. She didn't have to wait long. From out of the shadows she saw the unmistakably lean, gawky Luella, one of the slave girls on the Mitchell plantation.

"Luella, what in the world are you doing out here?" Anne asked.

Before she could question further, the girl ducked into the brush and disappeared back up the narrow trail. Anne knew what that meant. She was going back to the house to tell Anne's parents that their beautiful, raven-haired daughter was running off with her lover instead of staying at home to wed the man they'd arranged for her to marry.

There was only one thing to do now. Anne ran through the forest at full speed. Branches tore at her clothes and she barked her shins on jagged stones and low stumps, but finally she caught a glimpse of the lantern up ahead. Her love, John Bell Hood, was waiting just where he promised he'd be. As she approached, she could see him sitting on horseback. A second horse was saddled beside him, ready to go. *I'm going to make it,* she thought, her lungs burning and her heart pounding from the dash through the woods. *I'm going to be free after all.*

The night air was torn with the sound of a single gunshot. A warning. From somewhere not very far behind her, Anne heard the clatter and rumble of rapidly approaching hoofbeats. Another shot echoed into the night. She kept running. John saw her now and urged her onward.

"Anne, I'm here. Hurry, they're close behind."

Anne scrambled to his side and he grabbed her hand to help pull her up. Horses crashed into the clearing just as she made it into the saddle.

"Wait right there!"

It was Anne's father. He rode up quickly beside Anne's mount and grabbed the reins. Behind him Anne's brother, Stephen, was leading a group of the Mitchell family's hired hands, all armed and prepared to stop the young couple at any cost. The family name was at stake.

Anne and John sat in silence, defeated.

"Anne, we're going home now," her father said. He turned to his hired hands. "Gentlemen, escort Mr. Hood as far as the Montgomery County line and see that he's making his way safely back toward West Point. I'm sure the army can ill afford to lose such a fine soldier in these dangerous times, and I want nothing in Mount Sterling to delay his return to New York."

"Sir," John Hood interrupted. "You should know that I love her. Your daughter and I are in love."

"Thank you, Mr. Hood," the old man replied coldly. "I wish you safe travels. My daughter and I are returning home. I trust you've heard that she is to marry Thomas Anderson, a man of considerable means who is also quite fond of her. I'm sure you understand."

Her father pulled the reins of his daughter's mount and led her up the road back toward the Mitchell plantation. She would never see John Bell Hood again. As father and daughter plodded along slowly in the dark, she loosened her hair, which fell in thick black waves around her shoulders. She hung her head and sobbed from her heart. Was it really just a few months before that she'd been so happy, carefree, and joyously in love? she wondered. How had her sincere love for one man have gone so wrong?

The gardens that surrounded John Hood's family home, adjacent to the Mitchell property, were obscured by darkness as she and her father rode past. But it was easy to imagine them bathed in sunlight. The memories came flooding back. This was the place Anne and John cherished most. They'd spent hours on these garden paths walking and talking, their love growing with each word and every step. Many young men had pursued her as she blossomed into her teenage years, but Anne had only ever loved the tall, blond boy she'd known all of her life. John Bell Hood was her neighbor, her friend, and over time became Anne's one and only true love.

Anne knew the Hoods were not wealthy, like her family. John's father, Dr. John W. Hood, made a modest living teaching aspiring physicians and working his small farm. She had no interest at all in things like financial status or social standing. She also knew that such things ruled her parents' every action. Nothing was done in the Mitchell house without careful consideration of the effects it might have on the Mitchells' good name and the family bank accounts. She would let others worry about such things, she thought. She was in love with a good, honest, handsome young man who was on his way to West Point to become an army officer.

She thought she'd cared deeply for him before, but it really was that summer in 1849 when John came back from West Point on leave that their love truly blossomed. They spent most afternoons, and not a few stolen hours in the late evenings, meeting in these lush gardens on the Hood property, where their flaming passions fully kindled.

"I will love you forever," Anne had told John. "In this world or the next, I shall only walk the garden path with you."

The summer days and nights went by in a blur. John would be returning to West Point soon. He would return to marry her, he said. The plan was perfect but for two complications. Anne's father thought Dr. Hood a low-class pauper; by extension his son was little more than a country doctor's son and, now, a government servant. Anne's father began to complain about the amount of time Anne and the Hood boy spent together, saying there was surely no benefit to the Mitchells from such a relationship.

So Anne wasn't completely surprised when later that summer, a man named Thomas Anderson showed up at the Mitchell house clearly intent on courting her. She tried to show her disinterest by ignoring him. Anne's parents, who were smitten with Thomas's high Southern breeding and substantial family fortune, were enraged.

"This is a fine young man, a man worthy of your attention!" Anne's father had bellowed. "You're embarrassing the family behaving this way. Do you know what Thomas has agreed to do? If you marry him he will invest in our property and build you a magnificent home right here beside ours. Think about it, Anne. The Mitchell family would have the most glorious estate in the county. Can your West Point soldier provide anything even close to that?"

"And he's a handsome and gentle man, too," Anne's mother added. "You'll have beautiful children and he'll make a wonderful father. Anne, you'll be raising your family right here at home, near us. Isn't that what you want? What kind of life will you have as the wife of a military man?"

Anne was heartsick. She could see clearly where this was leading. Her family had already decided. She was going to be forced to marry Thomas Anderson.

"But I love John Bell Hood," Anne protested.

Her father stared at her in stony silence.

"It's not a wise choice," her mother counseled gently. "Think of the family."

John had returned to West Point, and Anne resisted as long as she could. But under intense pressure from her parents, she finally consented to marrying Thomas Anderson. She had one condition, she said.

"I must write to John and explain everything to him," Anne said. "He needs to hear this from me."

"It's not necessary," her father said. "It's not what a young woman does when she's engaged, to write love letters to another man."

"Then there will be no engagement and no wedding."

Her father weighed his options.

"Very well," he conceded. "Write your letter and let it be your last communication with this John Hood."

Anne poured her heart into the letter, professing her undying love for John and explaining how she was being trapped and manipulated into a loveless, passionless marriage. She would never forget the tall blond boy she loved, she said. And she would never, ever walk the garden path again. Her tears stained the paper as she finished.

"When you read this, know that I am longing for you and only you," she wrote. "And every time you revisit this letter for as long as you live, please know that it is, in that moment, still true. Yours in love always, Anne."

When John saw the letter, he was heartsick and enraged. In that moment of passion he hatched the doomed plan to return to Mount Sterling and wait for Anne in the woods with two horses and enough provisions for them to steal away together and be wed. It was that plan that now had Anne riding forlornly back to her home in her father's custody while armed men escorted John Bell Hood out of town.

"Why, Father?" Anne asked as they got back to the Mitchell home just after midnight. "Why do all of this when you know it wounds me so?"

"It's what is best," the old man said. "You'll see that someday. In our family we do what is best."

As they dismounted, Anne saw Luella peering at them from the side of the barn. Seeing that her work as a spy had been fruitful, the slave girl ducked back into the shadows timidly.

"Damn you," Anne muttered. "Damn you all."

After the failed elopement, Anne was locked in her room, a prisoner in her own home, until the wedding day. The ceremony came and went in a blur. Anne remained silent, stoic, as she took her vows and became Mrs. Thomas Anderson.

"You're a married woman now," her father said to her after the wedding. "Congratulations. You are, of course, now free to come and go as you please."

Anne said nothing. As soon as the guests had all gone home, Anne returned to the room she'd been sequestered in and there she remained, a silent recluse within the Mitchell estate. She passed her time ignoring her parents and her new husband and sitting by her window, looking across to the Hood family's gardens. She was miserable and she had no intention of letting anyone forget it. Thomas heaped affection and money on his new bride, but it did little to ease her depression and anger. She still would not speak.

The silence notwithstanding, the couple did spend enough time together to conceive a child. Anne suffered through a difficult pregnancy and harrowing labor. She took her new baby boy, Corwin Anderson, in her arms and spoke for the first time since her wedding day. The words cast a pall over the birthing room.

"A curse on all of you," Anne seethed. "A curse upon all who had any part in making me marry Thomas when my heart will always belong to John Bell Hood."

It took very little time for her curse to take effect. Less than three hours after the childbirth, bruised, purple clouds gathered in the western sky. All of central Kentucky braced for a late summer storm. A cold wind swept away the cloying, humid air and fat raindrops kicked up dust in the road around the Mitchell house. Rumbling thunder closed in; storm clouds obscured the afternoon sun.

"We'd better get these windows closed," one of the midwives said.

Without warning, the afternoon air exploded in a cobalt flash, as lightning struck the corner of the Mitchell home. The impact sent timber and brick raining down on the occupants of several of the rooms. Family members, hired hands, and slaves dug bare-handed through the rubble. But for three people in the Mitchell house, it was too late. In a pile of smoldering stones near the basement, they found the bodies of Stephen Mitchell, the brother who had led John Bell Hood away from Anne forever, and Luella, the slave who had tipped off Anne's father about his daughter's attempt to flee. And on the first floor, buried under tons of wood, brick, and mortar, was Anne herself. Her baby boy, Corwin, was less than four feet away, completely unharmed.

Six years after Anne was killed, Corwin told his father he'd seen his mother.

"She was walking in the flowers," the boy said innocently.

The words stunned Thomas Anderson. Corwin had been only hours old when she died. He couldn't possibly have any real memory of her. And Anne was rarely spoken of in the house, which had since been assumed by the Anderson family.

"What do you mean you saw your mother?"

The boy described Anne Mitchell-Anderson right down to the last detail. "She knew my name," the boy insisted.

But what sent his father reeling was where the boy saw her.

"She was walking in the garden path near Dr. Hood's house. She was looking for someone. I thought she was looking for me, so I ran to her. But she yelled at me and disappeared," the boy recounted.

"She . . . she spoke to you?" the father stammered.

"Yes. She said nobody could walk on that path with her. She was very angry. Then she was gone."

The story froze Thomas Anderson's blood. Earlier that day, Thomas Anderson had enlisted in the Confederate army. The appearance of Anne's ghost was a harbinger of doom, he was certain of it. It was. He left for military service with a sinking feeling in his gut. Within a month, he was officially reported as missing in action. He was never heard from again.

Corwin was raised by a series of nannies, servants, aunts, and uncles. Over the years he told them whenever he saw

Anne's ghost. The entire household had become much less dismissive since word throughout Mount Sterling was that the ghost of Anne Mitchell was roaming the Hood property and that the curse she uttered just before her death was in full effect. In both the Hood and the Anderson houses, tragedy was becoming part of the routine.

After Dr. John W. Hood passed away, the subsequent residents of the Hood residence were plagued with disastrous relationships and at least two suicides. In the Anderson home, the effects of the curse were far more profound. Corwin Anderson grew to be a prosperous Southern land baron like his father before him. By 1880 he had two strapping young sons, Isaac and English. They seemed a happy, healthy, and decidedly wealthy family. But Anne's curse wasn't done with the family, not by a long shot.

Isaac Anderson grew to be a gentle young man, well known around Mount Sterling for his generosity. English was his brother's exact opposite. He bullied the servants and terrified the neighbors around Montgomery County with his violent temper and disagreeable manner. It seemed, the good people of Mount Sterling said, like English Anderson was possessed by some angry spirit. Most attributed it to the curse his grandmother had uttered decades before.

"What do they mean when they talk about Grandmother's curse?" Isaac once asked his father. "Why is it like this?"

Corwin did his best to explain to his son the story of Anne Mitchell and John Bell Hood, right up to the botched attempt the couple made to run away together.

"So what became of John Bell Hood?" Isaac asked.

"The curse followed him as well," Corwin answered. "As much as she loved him, she still couldn't help making sure he was never truly happy without her."

John had continued to write to Anne for many years, not knowing that she'd died within a few years of their parting. The letters had been saved, giving the Andersons a fairly complete account of the young soldier's travels, Corwin said.

Fresh out of West Point, John served on the Texas frontier under General Robert E. Lee. At the time of the Civil War, he was a commander in the Texas Brigade. He fought at Gettysburg, where he lost an arm and a leg. But in 1864 he was disgraced when his troops were crushed in the Battle of Nashville, one of the worst Confederate losses in the war. He was drummed out of the military and went to New Orleans, where he tried to become a cotton broker. He also married a local woman and had ten children. But John wasn't much better at business than he was at commanding his troops. The family eventually went bankrupt. In 1879, thirty years after he'd tried to steal away with Anne in the night, John Bell Hood died of yellow fever. His wife died a short time later, leaving ten destitute orphans scattered around the country.

"What a sad tale," Isaac said.

"It is indeed, son," Corwin said, thinking about his own family's fates. "It is indeed."

Corwin sensed that what happened to John Bell Hood might be nothing compared to what Anne had in store for the family she despised most, the family still living in the home she considered her own. He was right.

In 1891, English Anderson flew into a rage over what he believed were intentionally undercooked potatoes. He confronted the family's cook in the kitchen. The cook apologized profusely but offered little in the way of additional satisfaction. English thought for a moment. Then, without warning, he grabbed one of the nearby carving knives and butchered the cook in cold blood. The case went to trial, but when the son of a wealthy landowner put his word against that of a hired hand, the jury determined that the attack was self-defense and turned English loose, much to the disappointment of many in the town.

It was a verdict that brought the full measure of Anne's curse home to the Anderson family. Shortly after the trial, Isaac, who had been surveying the property on horseback, rode up to his brother as he walked along the garden path near the old Hood property.

"Looking for Grandmother's ghost?" Isaac joked.

"Why don't you leave me alone and get back to your housekeeping?" English snapped.

Isaac could never understand the root of English's vile behavior. He'd always tried to be a good, loyal, supportive brother, but all he ever got in return was anger and bitterness. It seemed to flow from somewhere outside of English, as if he were a conduit for someone else's rage.

"That's why I'm here, actually," Isaac said, looking down from his mount. "I need your help. You'll need to get about twenty hands to repair the fencing in the southwest quarter. Can I count on you to do that?"

"Do it yourself! I have better things to do than to mend fences. That's why we have servants."

"Yes, but the workers need supervision and direction. You need to be there to guide them," Isaac said, an uncharacteristic anger now welling in him. He raised his voice a bit. "Please, English, I have a hundred other things I need to do. Take care of this."

Several field hands gathered around the brothers, attracted by the growing commotion.

English looked up at Isaac with eyes gone cold, vacant. He sneered at his brother. As the helpers stood by dumbfounded, English cursed his brother, but the voice that came out of the barrel-chested young man was, they said, clearly that of a woman.

"You Andersons still think you can make me do whatever you want, don't you? You don't control me, and you never have. Do you hear me? Never!"

English reached down and picked up a cobblestone. With all of his might, he hurled it at Isaac, striking his brother in the head and knocking him off the horse with a violent thud. Isaac was killed instantly.

When word reached the main house that English had killed Isaac, Corwin Anderson fell to his knees and howled in agony. He cursed the ghost of Anne Mitchell-Anderson, asking over and over, "Why do you still torment us?"

His burst of raw emotion past, Corwin asked to be taken to Isaac's body. He never made it from the house. As he descended the main stairs, he was gripped by a crushing pain in his chest and collapsed in a heap. Servants helped him onto a couch at the foot of the steps. It was too late. Corwin Anderson was dead of a heart attack brought on by the shock of his son's murder.

After the deaths, English Anderson's violence and rage blossomed unchecked. He seemed bent on destroying the Anderson family and its fortune. In 1901 he had a son of his own, Judson, but it did little to quell his antisocial behavior. The legend of Anne's curse grew as the people of Mount Sterling came to believe that English was the manifestation of the hatred the woman left behind. Fear of Anne's curse and of English Anderson's unchecked temper had folks giving the plantation a wide berth.

In 1911 English was doing business in the town when he began arguing with a merchant over the price of a recent delivery. As the merchant calmly tried to make his case, English pulled a knife and stabbed the man, killing him. When he returned home, he was met by a boy, the son of one of English's hired hands.

"There were men looking for you," the boy said.

"What men?" English asked.

"The police. They said you killed someone in town."

"Nonsense."

"Why, sir? Why do you do things like this? Why do you hate everyone so much?"

English towered over the boy, looking down on him with that same blank stare that came over him when he murdered his own brother. The voice that hissed from his lips was now strangely feminine.

"This is my house. Nobody else has any right to be here except me. I'm going to make you all understand that."

With his large, powerful hands, English Anderson beat and strangled the young boy, leaving his body in the dust of the courtyard. Now bloody from two murders in the past hour, he went into the house to wash. He would never come out alive.

A gathering mob of townspeople, already enraged by the killing of the merchant, descended on the Anderson property only to find the corpse of the servant's son. The vigilante crowd was now unstoppable. They burst into the house, chasing English through several rooms and halls before cutting him down with knives and axes. His butchered body was pulled along the paths around the house. In a final bit of impromptu shamanism, the mob even dragged his body along the garden paths at the edge of the Hood home.

They had, they reckoned, put the ghost of Anne Mitchell-Anderson to rest.

They were wrong. For the next thirty years, Judson Anderson, the last Anderson to live on the storied, ill-fated property, was haunted by dreams and visions of Anne's ghost moving through the halls of the house and the garden paths that separated the neighboring properties. Unable to cope any longer with the torment, Judson stripped naked and, carrying a pistol, waded waist-deep into one of the ponds that decorated the garden path. He fired a single shot into his temple, ending the Anderson legacy on that property forever.

To this day, townspeople still report seeing Anne's ghost in and around the old Mitchell and Hood properties. But these days her spirit has taken on a gentle nature. She's quiet, appearing thoughtful and not at all intimidating. Perhaps it's the way Anne always hoped to enjoy the garden paths, as a woman recalling her lover and the days they spent together basking in their romance. To do that, it seems clear, she had to rid the place of every last vestige of the family that took away her chance at true love. Now that they are gone, Anne's curse has become, to the great relief of the people of Mount Sterling, Kentucky, more like Anne Mitchell's garden of cherished memories.

Chapter 17

Visit at
Seamen's Bethel

It wasn't the only supernatural encounter of my life, but it was by far the most vivid. Could I get a message to a dead fisherman's mistress in time, and if I could, what in the world would it say?

It happened at the intersection of my two careers. In the fall of 1987, I was slugging it out as a city-beat reporter at a smallish daily newspaper in the gritty port city of New Bedford, Massachusetts. I was also a part-owner of a rapidly failing camera store. I'd gone in on the business with an old friend, a drive-time radio talk show host in the same town. We fancied that our celebrity status in the local media would make us a smash in the photography business. Turns out very few people cared at all.

I spent most of my days chasing car wrecks and fires and small-time political scandals. The camera store became a place to sit for four hours and write or make calls or daydream about making it big someday at the *Boston Globe*. I have no idea what my partner, Hal, thought about during his four hours in the shop every day. Maybe a network radio or television gig. But he was old, much older than me, in fact. He was on his second quadruple bypass when I met him. It's possible he spent his shift just happy to still be alive. I never asked. And it's too late to ask him now.

But while Hal was alive and I was still at least partially committed to the idea of entrepreneurship, we became very skilled at one particular photographic feat that managed to attract most of the money we made back then. I'd built a platform surrounded by brilliant and quite expensive color-correct lightbulbs. I'd fastened the guts of an old tripod perfectly perpendicular on one end so that when you attached a camera to the mount, you had a crisp, undistorted view of whatever was laid on the platform. This was Whaling City Camera's locally famous copy stand.

With that stand and the sophisticated Canon T-90 Hal owned, we could take crystal-clear pictures of pictures. Have a photo but lost the negative? Want to make enlargements of the photos in your high school yearbook? Looking for a poster made from the postcard you saved from your honeymoon? We could do all of that. When we started to offer the service, two things amazed me. One was how many people didn't keep the negatives for cherished family snapshots. The other was how badly most other camera shops reproduced old prints. Digital photography was in its infancy at the time, but because I had access to state-of-the-art workstations and software at the paper, I could not only make the quality of the copies better than the originals, I could also manipulate the images to remove flaws, distracting objects, and, more frequently, unwanted people.

You may not get rich in the photo business. But you will never go hungry if you can take ex-husbands out of family photos.

I was tired when I got to the camera store that morning in October 1987. I'd been in the newsroom most of the night, writing the story of a memorial service for two fishermen who'd been lost at sea a few weeks before. Family members had gathered in the Seamen's Bethel on New Bedford's Johnny Cake Hill to see the names of the lost men written on a new cenotaph, one of dozens that line the walls of the Bethel, memorializing the dead who sailed from New Bedford harbor and went to their final rest in the sea.

I'd interviewed a number of family members, including the captain's wife, a stern, stocky Portuguese woman who shared her memories of her husband in short bursts of broken English that sounded more like annoyance than grief. I thanked her and went back to look at the cenotaph, pretending to take notes. Actually I just stared at the names and wondered what it must be like to be a hundred miles offshore when twenty tons of steel-hulled trawler decides to head to the bottom of the ocean. It made me shiver.

I waited in the chapel until most of the folks had gone. There were just a few staffers milling about.

The Bethel was already twenty years old in 1851 when Herman Melville immortalized the place as the "Whaleman's Chapel" in his classic novel *Moby-Dick*. "In the same New Bedford there stands a Whaleman's Chapel, and few are the moody fishermen, shortly bound for the Indian Ocean or Pacific, who fail to make a Sunday visit to the spot," Melville wrote. It was no less true in 1987, though the trips were now to the rich fishing spots of the North Atlantic's Georges Bank rather than to the whaling grounds of the Pacific.

In the novel, Melville has the fire-and-brimstone pastor of the Seamen's Bethel preaching his sermon from a pulpit shaped like the bow of a ship. In fact, in the nineteenth century, the place looked pretty much like any other nondescript Puritan house of worship, right down to the plain, simple lectern. In 1961, a bow-shaped pulpit was added to match the description given in *Moby-Dick* to keep from disappointing the tourists.

I'd always liked Seamen's Bethel even though I'd never been out of sight of land for more than a few hours while fishing for summer flounder and stripers with my buddies. I liked it because it summed up what being from New Bedford was all about. Life. Death. God. Sea. I wrote that into my story about the memorial, then took it out. It seemed too obvious an observation for the folks who would be reading the paper the next day. They all lived with these things every single day.

So I was still drowsy and only half paying attention in the camera store the next morning when a woman walked in and asked to speak to Chris.

"That's me," I grunted. I looked up to see a rather striking older woman with flame-red hair and piercing green eyes. She was easily sixty-five years old, but she carried herself with all of the grace and elegance of the stunningly attractive woman she was accustomed to being her entire life. She was my grandmother's age and yet, I could feel myself blushing.

"Chris, my name is Maureen. I was told by a good friend that you can do some wonderful things with old photographs. I was hoping you could help me."

Her voice got softer and sadder with each word. This was some painful thing for her.

"I'll do my best," I mumbled, unsure of where this was all going.

She took a photo out of her handbag and slid it across the counter with one immaculately manicured finger. She wore a great deal of expensive-looking jewelry but no wedding ring. She smelled of fine powder and lilacs. I looked down at the photo.

"What do we have here?"

"It's me. A long time ago," she said, sounding a little defeated.

Indeed it was her. She was breathtakingly beautiful. She had a radiant smile. Given the clothes of the folks around her and the decorations visible in the background, the picture looked to be from the early 1960s.

"You'd like copies of this picture?" I asked.

"It's more complicated than that."

She reached back into her purse and pulled out a clipping from the newspaper I worked for. When she unfolded it, I felt my knees go weak. It was the obituary for the lost fishing captain, the one whose memorial service I'd covered the night before. A blurry black-and-white picture of the captain stared back from the rough newsprint. It wasn't much of an image, as obituary photos go, probably some small detail from a larger family portrait. Despite that, the handsome old captain's square jaw and bright eyes set off by a thick salt-and-pepper moustache were plain to see. I thought about his frumpy widow. An odd couple, to be sure.

"I wonder, Chris, if you could combine these two photos."

"You mean the picture of you and the obit from the newspaper?"

"Exactly."

I must have looked at her like she was stark raving insane, because she began to put the pictures back into her purse. She stopped and set them back on the counter with a long sigh, and started very softly, almost imperceptibly, to cry.

"I have never had to tell another living soul this," she said in a near whisper. "There's no reason I should have to tell you. It's none of your business. But I will. I'll tell you anyway.

"This man you see here, this dead sea captain? This is the man I have loved all of my life. We have been lovers since before you were born, Chris. Can you understand that? He was married. He had his family. And I was his mistress. And now he's gone. I have nothing at all of his, not even one photo of us together. That's all I'm asking. I'm asking you to make me one photo with us together that I can have . . . "

It finally became too much. She slumped over the glass store case and began weeping loudly, deeply. Here she was, a woman who had lost the man in her life but couldn't go to the funeral. She couldn't follow the family to the commercial pier to see the flowered wreath thrown into the sea in remembrance. She couldn't attend the memorial service at the Seaman's Bethel to hear the bell tolled in his honor and to see his name on the cenotaph. She couldn't mourn. She couldn't grieve. Until this very moment in my camera store.

She cried like that for close to twenty minutes. When she finally raised her head, the glass case and the newspaper clipping were soaked with her tears. I handed her a handkerchief. She dabbed at her eyes with it.

"I'm so sorry," she said.

"I'm sorry as well, ma'am. I'm very sorry for your loss."

The acknowledgment of her grief washed a calm over her. We talked for almost an hour about how they'd met, where they'd been, and how her love deepened even though she had him to herself only part of the time. She said she figured nobody would ever understand that. I told her she was probably correct.

She looked down at the ruined clipping of the obituary.

"I'll need to get another copy of the paper," she said.

"Actually, I work at the newspaper, Maureen. I can get as many copies of that obituary as you want. But here's the thing. I am not going to be able to make a very good composite of your color photo with this tiny newsprint picture. Surely you understand that."

"My friend says you do excellent work, Chris. I trust you to do your best." She pulled out a crisp $100 bill from her purse and pushed it at me with that same elegant finger. "I'll leave this with you as a deposit. When shall I call you?"

I had no idea how I was even going to begin this project.

"Tell you what, Maureen. Leave me your number, and I'll call you just as soon as I have something to show you. If it's progressing the way you want, fine. If you don't like the quality, I'll give you your pictures and your money back." I was banking on the latter.

She agreed and gave me her number. Then she floated out of my store as quietly as she'd entered. I'd never see her again.

Later that evening, I went to the paper to work the night shift, and right away started rummaging through the old papers to get a clean copy of the captain's obituary. The managing editor surprised me in the old newspaper archive, affectionately known as the morgue.

"Gonsalves, I have a sweet job for you!" he yelled. That usually meant some boring assignment or some menial office task. In this case, the latter.

"We fired the office assistant today," he went on. "Turns out she wasn't doing anything 'cept chatting with her sisters and doing her nails. Here."

He thrust an overstuffed manila envelope at me.

"What the hell is this, chief?" I asked. "I have other things to do here, you know."

"Yeah, well, add this to your list. The girl wasn't mailing the obit photos back to the families. We've got a month's worth of sacred family heirlooms here. I'm trusting you to get these mailed out so I don't have a whole bunch of grieving relatives storming my office looking for their snapshots. Got it?"

My mouth had gone dry. Did he say a month's worth of obit pictures? Was it possible I was holding an envelope that contained the original glossy color picture of the dead sea captain? If I was, I knew I'd be able to make a spectacular composite for my customer, the mysterious mistress. I was thinking now how handsomely she might pay for such a piece of work.

Meanwhile, my boss was expecting an argument. I disappointed him.

"Sure thing, chief," I said. I ran from the morgue back to my desk to see what was in the folder.

I found it easily. It was the eleventh picture from the top. Just as I'd suspected, the obituary photo had been cropped from a larger professional family portrait. In the sharp, color print the captain stood with that same broad smile, his arm draped over the shoulder of his wife, the woman I'd met at the memorial. They had three sons, who favored their father. And in this picture the sparkle in his eyes was set off by the craggy, weathered look of his handsome face. He looked every bit a man of the sea. Did he also look like a man who would enjoy the company of a gorgeous, flame-haired mistress? I suppose he did.

It would have been easy to simply take the photo back to the camera store for a day, shoot a copy of it, then mail the original back to the rightful widow. But I was in a quandary. Should I use the property of the man's wife to make a photo for his mistress? Fate, or something like it, had set the thing in my hands, but what was I prepared to do with it? I decided to take the photo with me for a walk in the cool autumn air.

New Bedford at night can be a glorious place. The lights begin on the horizon with the greens and reds of the buoys at sea and continue up past the gas lamps of the docks, eventually spilling all around your feet in crazy amber hues on the ancient cobblestones. My shoes clicked and clacked over the stones as I trudged up Johnny Cake Hill and stopped in front of the Seamen's Bethel. It didn't occur to me until I got to the front door that this was where I was headed. In those days, the doors to the Bethel were always unlocked. There was always one lone light on inside, for anyone who needed to pray for protection. Or in my case, guidance. I walked in and sat in the pew closest to the cenotaph that bore the name of the sea captain whose photograph I held in my hand. What happened next was so powerfully surreal that the memory of it is as if it happened to me in a childhood dream. Foggy. Distorted. Faraway.

I was sitting on the edge of the pew with my head bowed forward, the wood of the seat back in front of me cool and smooth against my forehead. I had my eyes closed. That's when I felt it. Like a cold wind pushing at my back. At first it was blowing against me, sending chills up and down my spine. Then it was coursing through me. I felt hollowed out as this force rushed and glowed inside me. It was lifting me out of the pew. There was no pain, but there was an overwhelming sense of confusion and frustration. I was completely disconnected from the reality of the bethel. I was now engaged in some sort of communication with this force that had gotten inside me. It struggled to find its voice to speak to me. I could feel its desperation as it tried to bridge the divide between us.

"Yes."

I heard it say the word. I felt it say the word. I understood it. The energy became calmer. More focused.

"Yes."

And shortly after that:

"Soon."

Yes and soon.

The energy rushed back out of me and I fell in a heap on the back of the pew. I was panting like I'd just run a mile at full speed. I tried to get my bearings. As I did, I noticed one of the bethel's hymnals was on the pew next to me. It hadn't been there before, I was certain. I'd have seen it. The book was sitting there on the seat facing me, opened to Hymn 241, "'Tis Midnight and on Olive's Brow." I stuck the picture of the captain and his family in that page, picked up the book, and left the bethel. I sang the old Protestant hymn to myself as I walked back to the office, trying very hard not to be spooked into a panic by what had just happened to me.

'Tis midnight, and on Olive's brow
The star is dimmed that lately shone;
'Tis midnight, in the garden now
The suffering Savior prays alone.

The next day, I got to the camera store early. Before I set up the copy stand, I decided to call Maureen. I wanted to tell her I'd come across the original photo of the captain.

But mostly I wanted to find a way to mention the encounter I'd had at the bethel. I wasn't going to tell her in detail, of course. But I did want to know what these words "yes" and "soon" might mean. I dialed her number. A man answered. When I explained who I was, he told me that Maureen had been taken to the hospital the previous day with a high fever. Kidney problems, he said. It was nothing serious. The doctors wanted to keep an eye on her, that's all. She'd be home in a few days. I thanked him and hung up.

I got to work on the photos, shooting multiple exposures of both pictures so I could match the light in the final composite. I developed the film and waited. When I looked at the negatives on the light table, I saw I had everything I'd need to make a nice keepsake. A few more hours on the computer and by the end of the day, I had what appeared to be a beautiful, candid snapshot of Maureen and the captain. In the picture, they were side by side, smiling broadly in a way they never could be in public. I made a half dozen eight-by-ten prints, brought them back to the camera store, and set them in the pick-up bin in an envelope marked with her name. By now I could see some of the shortcomings in the composite, of course. The two people weren't in precisely the same scale. The background transferred harshly from the party scene in her photo to the portrait backdrop in his. More important, the shadows were at slightly different angles on their faces. Still, all in all, I thought my customer would be pleased.

The next morning, I called her again. Her brother answered. Things had changed. Her fever wasn't coming down. She was going to be hospitalized for a few days. Nothing to worry about, just a small delay. I was disappointed.

Just before I left the shop for the day, the words "yes" and "soon" came creeping back to me. What could they mean? I took Maureen's envelope out of the bin and removed one of the prints. It seemed subtly different. Perhaps it was just the light, or maybe I'd been looking at the image too long, but it really looked like the difference in scale of the two photos had somehow been resolved. They looked more natural now. Sure, the background was still a bit messy and the shadows gave away the composite. Perhaps I'd done a better job than I had first thought.

I waited five days before I called Maureen's number again. Her brother sounded tired, distraught. His sister had a staph infection, he said. Her fever was raging. It didn't look good. I was dumbstruck. She'd been one of the most lively-looking women to ever grace my little camera store. I couldn't square my memory of her standing in my shop with the idea that she might be dying in a hospital bed somewhere right now.

I took her photos out again to look at them. This time there was no doubt at all about the change. It was no trick of light or error of perception. Not only were Maureen and her captain in perfect scale, but the distorted background had been smoothed and warmed into a perfectly unobtrusive backdrop. It was beyond my level of skill as a graphic artist to have accomplished what I now saw on all six prints in the envelope. What was happening? Yes? Soon? Where was this leading? I thought about the hymnal that wound up beside me in the bethel. I hummed the tune to myself. "'Tis midnight, and on Olive's brow . . . The star is dimmed that lately shone."

A weekend came and went. I took to calling Maureen's house daily, but now there was no answer. I called my contacts at the local hospital and they said she'd been transferred to a hospital in Boston. They didn't know which one. No help.

By Saturday of that week I was working the late shift again at the paper, helping out a buddy of mine on the copy desk, checking page proofs for the early edition. I scanned the obit page and my heart sank. There she was, Maureen, my customer, the captain's mistress. She was dead. I'd never get to show her the photo I'd made for her. She'd never get to see a happy image of her and her lover together . . .

And then it struck me. Yes. Soon.

I read her obituary to the end. It politely avoided the matter of her never having been married. It concluded that she was survived "by her brother, Francis, and her loving daughter, Olive."

'Tis midnight, and on Olive's brow
Is borne the song that angels know;
Unheard by mortals are the strains
That sweetly soothe the Savior's woe.

The camera store was closed on Sunday, but I went in and opened up anyway. I grabbed Maureen's envelope, not sure what I'd find there. The images were now stunning in their clarity. Scale, background, and even the shadows matched. There was nothing about these prints that would betray them as a composite. In fact, I'm no longer sure they really were a composite. I put the prints together in a fresh envelope and took them with me when I left the store. Monday, I left work at 2 p.m. and drove to the funeral home, where Maureen's wake was being held.

I spotted her immediately as I stood waiting in the receiving line beside the casket. She had her mother's red hair and delicate features, but she had the captain's bright eyes.

"Olive?" I asked, holding out my hand.

"Yes."

"I have something for you. It's from your mother. She wanted you to have these." I gave her the envelope with the prints.

"Should I open this now?" she asked.

"Soon," I said. I smiled at her. Then I left. I'll never know how she felt when she took out the copies of the only photo in the world of her mother and father together. In fact, I don't even really know what she saw when she looked at those prints. Was it the same thing I saw? I wasn't even sure what that was anymore.

Further Reading

Haunted Love owes a debt to countless paranormal investigators and writers who, through the ages, have tackled the often difficult task of rooting out the historical facts buried in the spooky legends, fables, and folklore that make up most ghost stories.

For even more detail on these and other stories, and to gain insight into some of the technical investigations into the paranormal activities surrounding them, the author wholeheartedly recommends the following:

IN PRINT:

Belanger, Jeff. 2005. *Encyclopedia of Haunted Places: Ghostly Locales from Around the World.* Franklin Lakes, NJ: Career Press.

My fellow Bay Stater Jeff Belanger has a dozen terrific books on the supernatural, including *Ghosts of War, Weird Massachusetts,* and *Who's Haunting the White House?* His most ambitious work, however, is this comprehensive directory, compiled from the writings of dozens of the world's leading paranormal investigators. Research notes, location background, firsthand accounts, and many anomalous photographs featuring ghostly manifestations make up the hundreds of haunted listings in Jeff's amazing collection.

Brown, Alan. 2004. *Stories from the Haunted South*.
Jackson: University Press of Mississippi.
Brown has collected more than fifty-three accounts of ghostly encounters from Alabama, Arkansas, Florida, Georgia, Kentucky, Louisiana, Mississippi, North Carolina, South Carolina, Tennessee, Texas, and Virginia, and he brings them to life with personal stories of ghostly encounters.

Cheiro. 2004. *True Ghost Stories*. Whitefish, MT: Kessinger.
Cheiro was a world-renowned seer, or sensitive, who was consulted by royalty and other famous people including Mark Twain. His predictions were rumored to be highly accurate. In this volume Cheiro chronicles some of the episodes of the paranormal that touched his life, like our story of the Ghost at the Throttle. The experiences related in this text served as the original and true predecessors to what have now become a vast store of ghostly lore.

Holzer, Hans. 1999. *Hans Holzer's Travel Guide to Haunted Houses: A Practical Guide to Places Haunted by Ghosts, Spirits and Poltergeists*. New York: Black Dog & Leventhal.
The only practical travel guide on the subject ever published, this book provides useful and current information on haunted places—complete with addresses, instructions for finding sites, historical background on the place and region, what to look for when you get there, and, not least of all, what to expect once you've had an encounter.

Kermeen, Frances. 2002. *Ghostly Encounters: True Stories of America's Haunted Inns and Hotels.* New York: Grand Central Publishing.
Herself the owner of a haunted inn in St. Francisville, Louisiana, the author discovered in 1980 what a boon to business a ghost could be. She then set out to document ghost sightings at more than 150 haunted inns and hotels across America, including places such as the Don CeSar Hotel. This book is packed with chilling stories along with practical information for those who want to spend the night in a haunted house.

Moran, Mark, Mark Sceurman, and Joanne Austin. 2006. *Weird Hauntings: True Tales of Ghostly Places.* New York: Sterling Publishing.
The same authors who brought us *Weird U.S.* have compiled stories about some of America's scariest haunted places, including haunted houses, ghostly graveyards, cursed roads, eerie eateries, spirited saloons, and more.

ONLINE:

Ghost Village (www.ghostvillage.com)
By far the Web's largest and most comprehensive supernatural community, Ghostvillage.com has more than fifty thousand pages of content with contributions by people from all over the world. Everyone from professional paranormal investigators to ghost witnesses to the simply curious can discuss ghost research, evidence, and supernatural points of view.

New England Paranormal (www.newenglandparanormal.com)

This is the official site for the group founded by noted celeb ghost tracker Stephen Gonsalves, who, despite having the same last name and coming from the same obscure little city in southern New England as yours truly, is no relation at all. Anyone who has met us both would know this. Stephen, who starred in the Sci-Fi Channel's reality show *Ghost Hunters,* has made-for-TV good looks. And I'm a writer. New England Paranormal is one of the more serious paranormal research, investigation, and documentation organizations. The site, with its repository of ghost stories and case files, is an excellent research resource.

Paranormal Research Society (www.paranormalresearch society.org)

Founded as a student club at Penn State University in 2001, PRS has grown into a professional organization dedicated to exploring the unknown. Its main mission is to "scientifically and spiritually explore" the supernatural. That and continue to produce their hit A&E series, *Paranormal State.* I always wonder if Joe Paterno knows about these kids.

The Atlantic Paranormal Society (www.the-atlantic-paranormal-society.com)

From the publishers of the popular *TAPS Paramagazine,* this is another respected paranormal research group that meticulously documents its work online.

The Shadowlands Ghosts and Hauntings (http://theshadow lands.net)

The Internet's original ghost story Web site, now with more than 13,800 real experiences shared by visitors and ghost hunters.

About the Author

Chris Gonsalves first discovered the power and romance of the spirits of the undead while working as a newspaper reporter on the historic cobblestone streets of New Bedford, Massachusetts. From the old ghosts of the widow's walks and seamen's memorials of the Whaling City, Chris moved on to the spooky world of magazine publishing, where he has served as an executive editor for a number of national consumer and business titles including *PC Week, Baseline, Gulfshore Life,* and *Newsmax,* covering everything from computers to fine food to fashion. He lives on Cape Cod, Massachusetts, and Palm Beach, Florida, with his wife and two dogs, who clearly are possessed by old, drooling demons.